Praise for William Bernhardt and The Florentine Poet

"Pietro's passion for his angelic Sophia mirrors the author's love affair with the written word....[T]his book sparkles like a jewel in a cosmic clockwork — an uplifting gift to readers everywhere."

DAN MILLMAN, NEW YORK TIMES-
BESTSELLING AUTHOR OF *WAY OF THE
PEACEFUL WARRIOR*

"Nothing short of brilliant. This is the author's love letter to poetry, words, and writing. It is also a tribute to all of those who help us along the way, and the lessons they teach us. Bernhardt's command of the written word is spectacular....It is the uplifting story we all need as this new year begins—let love conquer fear. *The Florentine Poet* is unforgettable.

DREAMSOFMANDERLEY (IG REVIEW)

"William Bernhardt is a born stylist, and his writing through the years has aged like a fine wine...."

STEVE BERRY, *NEW YORK TIMES-
BESTSELLING AUTHOR OF *THE LAST
KINGDOM*

"Bernhardt keeps his readers coming back for more."

LIBRARY JOURNAL

The Florentine Poet

The Florentine Poet

WILLIAM BERNHARDT

ILLUSTRATED BY
BRIAN CALL

BABYLON
BOOKS

For everyone who ever loved a poet

Poets are all who love, who feel great truths,
And tell them; and the truth of truths is love.

PHILIP JAMES BAILEY

One

Just before midnight, I learned why the churches in the San Frediano district are always closed on Christmas Eve.

I'd been in Florence for seven months. During that time, I filled each day with simple pleasures. I walked the Ponte Vecchio, Europe's oldest wholly stone, closed-spandrel, segmental-arch bridge. I cooled myself at the Fountain of Neptune and marveled at Michelangelo's David. I visited the Pieta at the church of San Lorenzo regularly. I indulged in a daily dose of gelato.

But I didn't write a single word.

I try not to romanticize the poet's life, rattling on about writer's block and the glorious struggle to find the *mot juste*, the lightning rather than the lightning bug. But as a poet with four published collections from Graywolf Press plus a Selected Poems edition from Villard/Random House, a poet twice named poet laureate of my home state, once of the United States, thrice nominated for the Pulitzer, I know this: when you lose the words, your life as a poet is over.

As evening came on this particular day, Christmas Eve, I sat at the desk in my garret at the Palazzo Magnani Feroni. I doodled, I stared out the window, I watched gulls soar across the Arno, I watched street workers decorate Christmas trees in the Piazza. But I wrote nothing.

I was terrified.

"Garret" might be somewhat misleading. The Palazzo Magnani Feroni is a spectacular hotel. According to the information in my room, the Palazzo was erected in 1428 and has been held by the same family for two-hundred-and-fifty years. Because that family previously dealt in antiques, the Palazzo is appointed with treasures that many a museum would be proud to display. The main entranceway, facing the via del Serragli, contains an arched portal incorporating the original ironwork of four knockers and a crescent moon, grounded by an ornamental wrought-iron gate crested with the Feroni coat-of-arms, which displays an armored forearm holding a sword and a gilded lily. The walls and ceilings bear well-preserved frescoes portraying scenes from Florentine medieval life.

The woman at the travel agency who recommended this hotel told me I made a wise choice. "It is a life-changing experience."

Exactly what I needed. Because I had not written anything for almost three years. And Christmas Eve looked no different than the many wordless days that had come before.

While I stewed in unproductive thoughts, I heard a knock on the door.

"Come."

I recognized the Italian woman who entered. She seemed to perform many functions at the Palazzo—she checked me in when I arrived, gave me directions the next day, and greeted me when I returned from my travels about town. She had lustrous ebony hair, an intriguing face, and spoke impeccable English.

"I have brought you soup," she declared.

I had to think a moment before replying. "I didn't ask for soup."

"It is a special holiday gift from the Palazzo." She stepped back into the hallway and wheeled in a cart. A domed silver tray rested in the center. She removed the lid to reveal a steaming tureen. "Minestrone. Like none you have ever tasted before. A specialty of the house."

"But...I didn't ask for soup."

"It is made from the finest ingredients. Beans, onions, celery, carrots, and tomatoes, all procured locally from Florentine farms."

I didn't want to seem ungrateful, but at that moment, when I was working so hard to produce a stanza, a line, or even a decent word, I saw this intrusion as an interruption to my writing— even though I was not writing. "I'm sorry. Thank you for being so thoughtful, but I'm not hungry."

"Everyone must eat. To nourish the body and soul."

"A writer must suffer for his art. A full belly is the artist's nemesis."

"As you wish." She wheeled the cart out and closed the door behind her.

I returned to my work. I could not fathom why the words had ceased to flow. Before, writing came as naturally to me as walking, more naturally than talking. I wrote my first poem when I was seven on the back of a Methodist church bulletin. I wrote because I was bored by the sermon, but my sweet mother praised the four-line doggerel and I've been writing ever since. Not a week of my subsequent life passed without a new poem springing forth from my pen. Not even while I was in college. Not even as I worked on my Master's degree.

Until now.

I touched the locket always in my pocket. Still there. Where were the words?

I passed some time on the phone. Nothing much had changed at home. My father and sister were well, though my father needed another knee-replacement operation. My editor

told me of the buzz in Manhattan, the *au currant* publishing
trends, the abysmal sales figures for her latest poetry book. My
agent reminded me that I was well past the delivery date for my
new collection and recounted the doomsday consequences that
would follow if my contract were cancelled for nonperformance.
Eventually I put the phone away and returned to staring out the
window.

There were no words.

I decided to venture out. Walking often stimulates inspiration. Rupi, Billy, Ted, and many others have written about this.
Perhaps a stroll to the Duomo and back would stir my blood. I
descended in the cage elevator and was almost out the front
door when I once again encountered the Italian woman. She was
tidying the lobby, but when I approached, she stilled her feather
duster.

"I have brought you a muffler." She reached into her leather
satchel and produced a long wooly scarf fringed at both ends.

"I don't wear a muffler."

"So I have noticed. That is my reason for bringing you one."

I didn't know what to say. "But…I don't wear a muffler."

"This is a lovely winter evening," she said. "The snow is just
beginning to fall. But there is a chill in the air. And you would
not wish to lose your voice on Christmas Eve."

"Very thoughtful of you. But the chill might do me good.
Comfort is not conducive to art."

"Neither is frostbite."

I took the muffler and stuffed it in my coat pocket.

"There will be a Christmas festival in the Piazza. Jugglers,
clowns, puppet shows. The festivities of the season. If you need a
guide—"

"Thank you. But I prefer to be alone with my thoughts."

"Everyone needs companionship."

"My companion is here." I tapped the side of my head.

She returned to her dusting.

I shambled into the street, ignoring the panic fluttering in my chest. I was barely aware of the people and places surrounding me. The sun sat low on the horizon, casting an orange-gold penumbra around the city. The snowflakes fell, light and brisk. They were more a visual embroidery than a weather condition. I buttoned my jacket and watched the sun descend, etching the outline of the cityscape like a Durer watercolor. I could see for miles around—the Duomo, the Church of Santa Croce, the Uffizi Gallery. My wordless friends of the past many months.

After pacing more than an hour I stepped inside a small bistro, ordered bottled spring water and a slice of pizza, then retrieved the Venetian leather journal and fountain pen I carried always.

I thought of the moonlight as it cast its spectral fingers across the city. I thought of the bustle of Christmas shoppers and the expectant eyes of children. I thought of the sound the Arno makes when it seems to be making no sound at all.

No words came.

After more than an hour of doodling, I returned to the Palazzo.

That woman was behind the front desk. I tried to make my way to the elevator without being noticed, but she spotted me before I could open the wrought-iron door.

"I have brought you a drink," she proclaimed.

"I don't drink. Alcohol interferes with the artist's—" I stopped short. She reached back to a hot plate on the credenza and returned with a steaming mug of what smelled like hot chocolate. "Oh."

"Just a little something to take off the chill."

I sipped. The drink tasted warm and doubly rich. Just the way I liked it. "Thank you, but I should—"

"Have you been to the rooftop terrace?"

"No."

"Not in seven months? That is a pity. So lovely there. Best

view in the city. And tonight, all the lights of Christmas will be ablaze. Some have said it is the most spectacular view in Italia. And the space heaters will keep you warm."

"Thank you, but—"

"There will be other guests there, passing the time. Since they are far from home and the churches are closed, they choose to socialize. Drinks and small snacks will be available."

"I already ate."

"But surely you don't want to be alone. On Christmas Eve?"

"Thank you, but writing is a lonely profession." I pushed the mug back to her. "This is the life I have chosen and I must be true to it."

She returned her attention to the register.

In my room, I gazed out the window at the twinkling holiday lights and inevitably thought of my mother. She loved Christmas, with all the trimmings. Tree, ornaments, lights, church service, huge meal, more gifts than any child needed or we could afford. Once when I was about five, she held me in her lap and said, "Darling, promise me you'll never marry a girl who doesn't like Christmas. You'll be sorry if you do." Once in church, when a preacher was talking about the miracle of Christmas, she whispered to me, "Every day is a miracle. You just have to open your eyes and see the wonders the angels have brought you."

I missed her so much. And I suddenly and desperately did not want to be alone.

I found the staircase that led to the rooftop terrace. I climbed three flights of stairs, which seemed at least six because the passage was old and narrow and difficult even for a man of slender build and decent health. The terrace was a stucco expanse yielding the promised spectacular view of the city and filled with many people in evening attire. I tried to be sociable. A woman in a red dress and a Babbo Natale cap took an interest in me. Small talk ensued. She seemed tipsy and a little bored. I felt certain she was about to move on when I let it slip that I was a poet.

Her eyes lit. "Have I heard of you?"

I've heard this question a thousand times but I still haven't managed to come up with an appropriate response. "How would I know?" sounds rude. Instead, I told her my name.

Her elbow slipped off the bar. "You're messing with me."

"No."

"You wrote 'The Other Door.'"

I feigned a smile. That poem made me famous, if any poet today can be considered famous. *The New Yorker* ran it first, then it was widely reprinted, blogged about, given its own Facebook page. On YouTube, you can find three-year-olds reciting it.

"Yes, I wrote that poem," I said, "and about four hundred others."

"That poem changed my life."

I've heard that one a thousand times, too. How do you respond? "Thank you?" "I'm glad?" "Changed for the *better*?" The poem is a longish character piece I wrote while my mother was dying of leukemia. The poem's voice is her voice. I can't read it without thinking of her. It's an extremely intimate work for me, and I've never become accustomed to having strangers who never knew her act as if the poem belongs to them.

"I've read everything you've ever written," the woman said, but as we talked further, it became clear that the only thing of mine she had ever read was 'The Other Door.' This was also not a new experience.

I felt foolish. I should never have come here. And all at once I knew where I wanted to go. I paid my tab.

"Are you leaving us?" the woman asked.

"I've always loved going to Christmas Eve church services. Ever since I was a child. I haven't done it in years, but I want to do it tonight."

"Are you afraid Santa won't fill your stocking if you don't go to church?"

I shrugged. "Most of the year I never even think about church. But I want to go now."

I tore down the stairs as quickly as the tight passage would permit, ripped through the courtyard, bolted across the lobby, raced out the front door.

I ran down the via del Serragli until I spotted two ornately carved heavy-oak gothic doors. I pulled on the handles.

The church was closed.

No matter. In this town, the next church was never far away. I continued running till I came to the Chapel of San Pedro, but again the doors were locked tight. No sign of anyone inside.

I checked every church in the San Frediano neighborhood, every chapel or cathedral on this side of the Arno. Without finding a single light on.

I stared at the locked doors, perplexed. In this famously devout country, why would all the churches be closed?

A memory flickered in my mind. What was it the woman at the front desk had said? *Since they are far from home and the churches are closed, they prefer to socialize.*

I stumbled back to the Palazzo. I looked for that woman so I could ask her about the churches, but for once she could not be found. I mounted the stairs to the terrace, now deserted. I sat alone in a chair in a corner, at a loss as to what to do next. I was not surprised to discover that I could not put my feelings into words.

"Excuse me."

I started. The man appeared beside me without a sound, as if he had materialized from the evening mist.

"I am Dr. Alberto Giannotti, the owner and proprietor of the Palazzo."

Even in the fading light, I could see he was a distinguished, handsome man. Though elderly, he seemed healthy and bright-eyed, with a ruddy complexion. He slicked his hair back in a manner reminiscent of a silent-movie playboy. His suit seemed perfectly tailored, with flared collars revealing a silk argyle ascot. He was the sort of man who made an immediate impression, a man who exuded graciousness, a man whose every gesture evidenced character and elán.

I took his hand. "Pleasure to meet you."

"The pleasure is mine. I thank you for staying at my ancestral home." He hesitated for the barest of seconds. "Forgive me, my new friend, but you seem...troubled. Is there anything I could do to assist you?"

I wasn't sure where to begin. "I'm...mystified."

"But by what?" His English was clear, spoken with a pleasing and unobtrusive accent. "The beauty of the countryside? The splendor of Florence?"

"I'm mystified about why all the churches are closed."

"Ahh." A small smile fluttered across his face. He gestured toward the opposing chair. "This is not something that can be explained hastily. May I join you?"

"Of course." I had no idea what his interest in me could be. Simply a gracious host, I supposed.

"The churches are closed on Christmas Eve throughout the San Frediano district," he began, gazing upward. "Elsewhere, in the tourist districts, of course, you may find churches open, but here they are closed because...well, I suppose you could say it is because of poetry."

I inched forward. "Poetry?"

"A form of verse characterized by metaphoric language selected for its euphony and suggestive power."

"I know what poetry is. I'm a poet myself. But what has that to do with the churches?"

"The churches are closed as a matter of tradition. A tradition that dates back to the fifteenth century. And a particular poet."

"Who would that be?"

"You do not know him."

I smiled. "I have a Master's degree in literature. I was poet laureate for a time in my home country. I suspect I'll know your poet."

"You do not," Giannotti replied. "And yet, he is the reason the churches are closed. It is a tribute."

"And why should these religious institutions make a tribute to a poet? On the eve of the most celebrated Christian holiday?"

Giannotti's answer was direct and unequivocal. "Because he was the greatest poet who ever lived. And because his tragic sacrifice is the only reason this city is here today."

Two

"The greatest poet who ever lived? Since we're in Florence, I assume you refer to Dante." I had seen the portrait by Giotto in the chapel of Bargello Palace.

"No. Dante is 47th."

I blinked. "I beg your pardon?"

"Dante Alighieri had a fine way with words, and *La Divina Commedia* has several passages of interest. Elsewhere, I know Dante is often referred to as *il Sommo Poeta*. But here in Florence, he is 47th."

"47th? *Dante?*"

"It is a respectable position. He has a ranking, on the extended list. Although typically one is not truly considered to be on the list unless one is in the top fifteen."

"So let me see if I understand you properly. Dante Alighieri, the author of the one hundred cantos of *The Divine Comedy*, doesn't make the top tier?"

"Elsewhere, certainly. But in Florence?" Giannotti smiled. "We take our poetry very seriously."

"I can't believe there are forty-six poets greater than Dante anywhere."

As Giannotti leaned back, French cuffs peeked out from his

blue sports jacket. His cufflinks were emblazoned with the Feroni coat of arms. "My friend, you appear to have a few moments to spare. Let me tell you a story."

"Will this explain why the churches are closed?"

"No. But it will explain why Dante is only number 47. Do you know the poet John Keats?"

"Of course I do. I have—"

"Yes, yes. A Master's degree in literature. Very impressive. Did you know that Keats once came to our fair country?"

"Certainly. He died in Rome near the Spanish Steps. I've been in the house. I've seen the room where he died."

"And bought the souvenir t-shirt, I'm sure. But did you know that before he settled in Rome, he spent a week in Florence?"

"I don't recall reading about that."

"It does not appear in the history books. But the people of Florence have a long collective memory."

"Why would Keats come here?"

Giannotti shrugged. "It is the most natural of things. That the acclaimed poet should wish to visit the city that gave birth to poetry."

"Wait a minute..."

"The city that gave life and breath to the form. The city whose name is synonymous with poetry in the hearts and minds of the citizens of the world." A huge generous smile spread from one side of his tanned face to the other. "Let me tell you what happened. And please remember that this occurred in the eighteenth century. Florence was the most sophisticated, most artistic, most splendid city in Europe. Artists, artisans, celebrities, and princes all wanted to be in Florence. Including Keats. He was ill with tuberculosis, probably caught while nursing his brother Tom. His doctors hoped a change of climate might improve his health. What better tonic could there be for a poet than Florence?

"And so Keats left behind his beloved Fanny Brawne, accompanied by his close friend John Severn. His reception in Florence was tremendous. Shops closed. Workmen took the day off. Teachers stopped teaching and bakers stopped baking. The city shut down completely and all its citizens turned out to see the famed poet. When Keats emerged from his carriage, he found himself greeted with cheers and singing. As he entered the Piazza della Signoria, Keats was visibly moved. Though frail, he drew himself up to his full height, tossed away his cane, and held out his arms as if to embrace them all. He spoke a few words of greeting and received thunderous applause. The lace handkerchief darted from his ruffled sleeve on several occasions as the great poet dabbed tears from his eyes. It was his proudest moment."

"I'm surprised I haven't read of this," I said with a decided edge.

"Keats spoke a few words. As it happens, I have committed them to memory. He said: 'Good people. I most humbly offer my thanks for this fine reception. It gratifies one who has given his all to the poetical arts to know that here, in Firenze, the majesty of the written word is so respected. I herewith promise that my next work, whatever it is and whenever it may be composed, shall be dedicated to you, and this city, and the nobility of spirit I find enshrined here.'

"Once again the poet was cheered with such enthusiasm that many wondered if the throng would ever let him depart. But eventually, as it became clear that he did not intend to say more, the people dispersed. Keats attempted to rejoin his friend waiting in the carriage. An elderly gentleman by the name of Antonio tapped him on the shoulder and asked if he would be kind enough to appear that evening at the final ceremony of Florence's Poetry Olympiad."

"Did I hear you correctly?" I asked. "A poetry Olympiad?"

"Have you never heard of it in your, um, literature department?"

"Poetry is not a competitive sport."

"Perhaps not where you come from. But here in Florence, we take our poetry very seriously. Shall I continue?"

I nodded. Resistance seemed futile.

KEATS, STILL BUOYANT FROM HIS GLORIOUS RECEPTION, AND undoubtedly feeling he must be the most beloved writer on the face of the earth, agreed to attend. The ceremony was held in the Santa Maria del Fiore, what you would call the Duomo, because as you shall learn, in Florence, poetry is considered a divine gift, and the connection between poetry and religion is close indeed. Keats listened patiently as the awards were distributed. Afterward, the master of ceremonies, a tall man named Vincenzo, asked the visiting poet if he would recite. Keats graciously agreed to do so. He eased his fragile body toward the podium and began:

"My heart is sad and armed with seas of pain—"

In the front row, Vincenzo winced.

Keats saw, but ignored it and continued: "I feel as if a poison made me ill—"

This line was greeted with groans, and not just from Vincenzo.

Keats never possessed any facility for suppressing his emotions. Especially irritation. "Is something the matter?"

Antonio, the older gentleman who had invited him, spoke first. "We are troubled by the inaugural line."

Keats dipped his chin. "May I inquire as to the cause for your concern?"

Antonio shrugged. "Doesn't quite work, does it?"

"Bit of a mixed metaphor, actually," Vincenzo added.

"Do tell." Keats batted his eyelashes at an accelerated rate.

"You don't arm yourself with seas, do you? You arm yourself with a sword or a dagger. You can be drowned by seas or soaked by seas. But armed with seas of pain?" He made a clicking sound with his tongue. "Just doesn't work."

Keats drummed his fingers on the podium. "Since you appear to have an expertise that far exceeds my own humble abilities, may I ask what you would suggest?"

Vincenzo didn't hesitate. "How about: My heart aches, and a drowsy pain engulfs…"

"Oh, much better," Antonio said, clapping his hands. "A thousand times improved."

"What if we created a paradox?" a large man suggested eagerly. He wore a beard longer than his neck and was called Johannes. "Perhaps the speaker feels both joy and pain. Or he feels both drowsiness and a powerful alertness."

"An oxymoron!" a young man named Federico shouted. He could have been no more than seventeen. His eyes were wild with excitement.

All the poets crowded together enthusiastically, for as all writers know, revision is where the magic happens.

"I've got it!" Vincenzo cried, snapping his fingers. "How about: My heart aches, and a drowsy numbness pains."

"Beautiful," his friends agreed. "Complex. Lyric. Ambiguous."

"And then for the second line, perhaps: My sense as though of hemlock I had drunk."

"Bravo!" the senior poets cried. "Bravo, bravissimo!"

Behind the podium, Keats tilted his head to one side. "Not… entirely unsound," he muttered. "Though perhaps a trifle over-wrought." But the observant noted that he was jotting down every word they said. "How can I repay you for this service?"

"Don't even think about it." Vincenzo shrugged. "Profes-sional courtesy."

"Are you all practitioners of the poetical arts?"

"Indeed," Vincenzo replied, without a trace of ego or preten-tion. "We are card-carrying members of the Poets' Trade Guild."

"Florence has a guild for poets?"

"But of course. Is there not in your land?"

"No. But perhaps I shall propose it upon my return. Would you mind terribly if I asked to hear some of *your* poetry?"

They readily agreed. After all, who can resist the opportunity to share what they love most? When Antonio and Federico and Vincenzo and Johannes read their poems, they were like proud papas displaying portraits of their children. Since he was the master of ceremonies, Vincenzo began, with a lyric tour-de-force involving the Duke of Florence, a swan, and a flying gondola. It was only a fourteen-line sonnet, but Keats was visibly moved. The elderly Antonio recited next, his voice trembling. He delivered a dark narrative poem about the fire of 1499, filled with foreboding and a brilliant bit of synecdoche in which a single flame represented all of perdition.

Keats's wheezing respiration quickened. His hand went to his chest, as if attempting to contain his rampant emotions.

Johannes recited a tribute to his mother, a masterpiece in which the woman who gave him birth was described in no fewer than sixteen successive independent clauses. Keats was so affected, not only by the vast technical prowess but by the stark emotional content, that he asked for a chair. He felt his legs could no longer support him.

And then young Federico delivered a poem he had composed just that morning.

Keats wept.

When at last he recovered himself, he grasped young Federico's hand and said, "What a prodigy you are. I thank heaven I was permitted to meet you before I pass from this earth. Surely you must be the greatest poet alive today."

"Oh no," Federico said, in the most matter-of-fact manner. "I am but 62nd."

"62nd?"

"Of the living poets. In the historic pantheon, of course, my number is much higher."

"But what poet could possibly be greater?"

"I'm 33rd," Vincenzo said, proudly jabbing a thumb toward his chest.

"And I am twelfth," Johannes said.

"I am second," the elderly Antonio creaked. "But I hope to improve myself."

"How can this be?" Keats implored. "Why have I never heard of any of you? Why have I never read your work?"

"We do not publish," Vincenzo explained.

"Whyever not?"

"Whyever should we? We do not seek fame or fortune. Poetry is a thing of grace and beauty, not a commodity to be bought and sold."

"But then—has the world no opportunity to experience the majesty and joy that your poetry brings?"

"We recite our work in the churches of the city. It is always well-received. That is enough for us."

GIANNOTTI REMOVED A HANDKERCHIEF FROM HIS POCKET AND dabbed his eyes. "Keats was floored. He shook their hands with an intense fervor and left the premises without speaking another word. Perhaps he was frightened by the magnitude of the talent surrounding him. Sadly, he passed soon after, never having a chance to write the work he promised to dedicate to the people of Florence. But one cannot help but wonder if he was thinking of his experience with the Florentine poets when he insisted that his epitaph should be: 'Here lies One Whose Name was writ in Water.'"

I arched an eyebrow. "And the point of this picaresque fairy tale?"

"The point, my friend, is that your critics and professors only know what they have read in books, and thus have missed some of the greatest poets who ever lived. And that is why to some, Dante is the supreme poet, but here in Florence, he is only 47th."

"Your story is absurd," I said. "That poem you quoted is 'Ode to a Nightingale,' the greatest of Keats' six great odes. And you're suggesting that it was actually written, at least in part, by a committee of Florentine Trade Guild members? That Keats stole his best poem?"

Giannotti raised a finger. "In the words of the immortal Stravinsky, 'Great artists steal. Bad artists borrow.'"

"'Ode to a Nightingale' was written on Hampstead Heath more than a year before Keats' death."

"So Severn wanted people to believe. He was quite protective of his friend's professional reputation."

"If Dante is 47th, and Keats is, oh, I don't know, somewhere in the three-digit numbers, who's number one? Who is this person you mentioned before who is the greatest poet who ever lived?"

"That would be Pietro Begnini, born here in Florence in 1459."

"Never heard that name in my entire life."

"I know, and that is a pity. If you knew his tale, you would not merely understand the mystery of the closed churches. You might understand…even more."

"Well then. By all means. Tell me."

What follows is the story of Pietro Begnini, just as Giannotti told it to me on the terrace of the Palazzo Magnani Feroni on Christmas Eve. He may have modernized the language, massaged a few of the details, embellished here and there. But the story is true, nonetheless. You may not believe it. But the people of Florence do. And now, so do I.

Three

I t is often said that writers are born, not made, and never was that truer than in the case of Pietro Begnini. According to his parents, the first words he spoke were in iambic pentameter. Although his baby talk made no sense, listeners still found themselves transported by the assonance and alliteration. Even his early tentative steps possessed meter and cadence. And his voice had a lyrical, mellifluous quality that entranced those around him.

When the boy was still in his cradle, he was visited by three wise men from the State Office of Poetry. They traveled from Rome to visit this strange but blessed child. One of them was Mario Morelli, also known as the Bard of Bertarelli Castle. Tradition holds that he placed his hand on the young infant's forehead and made the sign of the sonnet, forever anointing him and transferring his knowledge of the poetical arts to this newborn prodigy.

Young Pietro's parents were not artists. His father, Sal Begnini, had a vegetable stand in a local bridge marketplace. It was similar to Ponte Vecchio, but less pricey. Pietro's mother, Beatrice, handled the financial aspects of the business, for while Sal was popular with the farmers and the customers, numbers floated through his head like feathers on a windy day. Both parents enjoyed poetry, as enthusiastic lay people, but it played no great role in their lives. When they were informed that their child showed poetical promise, however, Beatrice resolved that they would do everything they could to support him. Even though she might not have chosen a career in the arts for her only son, she loved him without reserve and wanted him to find his own best destiny.

On Pietro's twelfth birthday, Sal took him to a meeting of the Florence Poets' Trade Guild and explained the situation. The Guild elders were understandably dubious. At that time, young Pietro was a dark, pudgy-faced boy with curls down to his nose and, it must be said, a fairly foolish expression that seemed permanently etched upon his face. Which is not to say that Pietro was foolish—far from it. Nor was he timid, as poets often are. But his face, through no fault of his own, was not one that inspired confidence. He looked like, to use a technical term often employed by Florentine artists, *tingeretti*. This is an Italian word which has no English equivalent but is perhaps most closely translated as: *doofus*.

"So you believe this child could be a poet?" asked the Grand Inquisitor. The Inquisitor not only led the Guild but also the great Academy of Florentine Poetical Arts. He wore long flowing black robes and an equally black skullcap. His hands always seemed to be out of sight. The High Council of the Guild also sat in audience that day, in their chairs in the elevated semi-circular dais where they held their meetings.

"I know nothing of poetry," replied Sal, slapping his son on the back. "But my boy has the blessing of the poet laureate and he speaks with a voice like none I have ever heard before."

"And I suppose you believe that if he were given an apprenticeship, he might secure a sinecure such that you would no longer have to spend your days peddling rutabagas."

Sal shook his head. "I know nothing about the Guild and sinecures."

"Indeed," the Inquisitor said, with obvious skepticism. He proceeded to ask many probing questions, fulfilling his inquisitorial function. You may wonder why a poetical society would have a Grand Inquisitor. You must understand that in Florence in the fifteenth century, poets were held in such esteem that they were not only considered among the most prominent citizens but were also rewarded handsomely. In the eyes of this society, being a poet was more prestigious than being a doctor, or a lawyer, or an investment banker. A position with the Guild was so potentially lucrative that they were virtually assaulted by pretenders and poetical messiahs, leading them to create a strict vetting program. In that year alone, the Grand Inquisitor weeded out more than three hundred unworthy contenders, and he was only known to have erred once, when he spurned Vasco de Como, the Troubadour of Tuscany. But that is a story for another day.

"I suppose you will claim to know nothing of the patronage a poet can secure. The court commissions. The fame, the glory, the endorsement deals?"

"Indeed I do not," Sal said, shrinking a bit. "I only want what is best for my boy."

"If I had a florin for every time I've heard that," the Inquisitor replied, "I would be a wealthy man."

"But, sir," Sal said, "you *are* a wealthy man."

The Grand Inquisitor rolled his eyes. "It was a rhetorical statement. Hyperbole."

Sal fell silent, but young Pietro did not.

"Pardon me, O Great One," the young boy said, in a voice as calm and smooth as the sea at night. "But you are incorrect."

The Inquisitor's eyebrows rose almost to the ceiling. "Me? Incorrect?"

"Your statement was not hyperbole," Pietro continued. "Hyperbole is a rhetorical device which deliberately exaggerates conditions for emphasis or effect. You probably exaggerated the number of times you have heard fathers expound upon their desire to seek what is best for their children, but your later comment was closer to irony or sarcasm, since you were implying that you were not wealthy when in fact you are one of the wealthiest men in the city."

"How dare—"

"But in truth, your remark is probably more accurately classified as sardonic, rather than sarcastic, since your protestations of lack of wealth not only emphasize the well-known fact that you are quite rich but also contain the unmistakable implication that the person to whom you are speaking is not wealthy and also not very smart. Wouldn't you agree?"

The Inquisitor glared. The High Council gaped.

They were dumbstruck for several reasons. First, no one ever spoke to the Grand Inquisitor that way, at least no one who hoped to live a long and pleasant life. The Inquisitor had more power than the Duke of Florence. His tendrils extended into every aspect of Florentine life—artistic, commercial, and religious. No one had spoken honestly to him in over thirty-two years, since the time he competed for the title he now held and he—

But we will return to that subject later.

The second reason the Council gaped was that, as was immediately clear to everyone present, Pietro was right. That the Grand Inquisitor would make such a grave error with regard to rhetorical devices was shocking. That he would attempt to have such sport with an uneducated grocer was a sign of great deficit of character. That his errors would be pointed out by a young boy of twelve was nothing less than earth-shattering.

But the third and final reason they gaped was Pietro's voice. His vocal timbre had matured since infancy. His voice had recently changed, and it was now rich with lyrical, dulcet qualities. His voice, though tinged with a slight lisp and a tendency to drop 'r's, commanded attention. Though it emerged from the face of a doofus, his voice offered a glimpse of paradise. This voice, they realized, was meant to speak poetry.

The Grand Inquisitor was not one who could be corrected and take it with good humor. He immediately interrogated Pietro about all things poetical.

"What is metonymy?"

"Metonymy is a metaphorical device in which an image is based upon something with which the actual subject is closely associated but is not actually a part thereof, as when people say, 'You can't fight the Poets' Guild,' but what they really mean is 'The Grand Inquisitor of the Poet's Guild is—'"

"What is apophasis?"

"Emphasizing something by ignoring it."

"Epizeuxis?"

"Repetition of a single word."

"Catachresis?"

"An exaggerated, implied metaphor using words in an unexpected manner."

No matter how many terms the Grand Inquisitor tossed out, he could not stump the young twelve-year old. His irritation increased with each failed attempt. Soon the elders of the High Council joined in, but they could not pose a question the boy could not answer.

"How many feet in a sonnet?"

"Seventy, obviously," the boy said, without pretense or show. "Fourteen times five."

"Syllables in a haiku?"

"Seventeen."

"Statement: The Duke is the best ruler ever. Problem: Give me the *dirimens copulatio*."

"'The Duke is the best ruler ever, but no duke is perfect.' That would be the balancing fact that prevents the statement from being one-sided or unqualified." At this point, Pietro almost seemed bored.

"Inconceivable!" the Grand Inquisitor bellowed. "This stripling cannot possibly know so much. He is cheating!"

The leader of the High Council frowned. "How would that be possible?"

"I don't know. But it must be so." He pointed a finger toward Sal. "His father must be helping him. Feeding him the answers."

"Surely you jest," Sal replied. "I haven't understood a word you've said since 'Good morning.'"

The Grand Inquisitor was a man of bad temper—that was almost an essential attribute in his line of work. But his frustration with Pietro, and his inability to expose the boy as the fraud he knew he must be, caused him such consternation that his face turned as black as his robes. He clenched his fists, snarled, and even uttered an oath in the name of Saint Columba, the patron saint of poets.

The Inquisitor leaned so near that Pietro could tell he had consumed much garlic at luncheon. "I will expose you, young whelp. Of that you may rest assured."

Fortunately, the members of the High Council, some of whom were not preternaturally mean-spirited, had a different reaction. They applauded, sang Pietro's praises, and cheered him. The leader composed an ode in his honor on the spot. They predicted that people would talk for years to come of the day when twelve-year old Pietro visited the temple of poetry and confounded the elders.

"So," Sal said hesitantly, "when the boy comes of age, does he have your leave to apply for admission to the Academy of the Florentine Poetical Arts?" Sal had been informed that completion of the Academy course was a necessary prerequisite to membership in the Poets' Guild.

The Grand Inquisitor started to object, but before he could speak, the leader of the High Council replied. "Your son does not even need to apply. Just bring him. Bring him on the first day of his eighteenth year. Please."

The Grand Inquisitor's face contracted.

"I will," Sal said, taking his boy by the hand. "Thank you. Thank you very much."

And so Pietro was set on the path to his future. From that day forth, his parents basked in the pride of knowing that one day their son would be a famous and successful poet. Pietro studied diligently, and he composed a sonnet, ode, or ballad every day. When the fateful birthday at last arrived, he was prepared to embark upon the glorious career they all thought inevitable.

Not one of them realized how horribly wrong they were.

Four

D r. Giannotti signaled toward the bar. "A Sambuca Molinaris, please." He looked at me sheepishly. "I fear my story will take longer than you may have anticipated."

Somehow, I was not surprised to find the drinks were brought by the dark-haired Italian woman I had already encountered three times that day. The woman with the soup, the muffler —and the terrace recommendation. Nor was I surprised to find that she had brought me hot chocolate, without my asking for it.

"This is Chiara," Giannotti explained. "She tells me the two of you have already exchanged a few words. She will be our server tonight."

"I will," she said, placing the drinks on the table between us. "But please remember the performance. I must be off before midnight."

"I shall not forget." Giannotti downed his Sambuca in a single swallow. "Shall I continue the story?"

I took my warm drink and cradled it in my hands. "Please."

❧

WHEN HE WAS BUT THIRTEEN YEARS OF AGE, PIETRO COMMITTED A terrible deed, the worst he would ever commit in his entire life, save one. He threw a rock at a dog. Worse, he lied about it afterward. To be sure, the dog was ferocious and possibly rabid, but the boy was in no immediate danger. The dog belonged to Francisco the Fruit Seller, who had the stall on the bridge adjacent to Pietro's father. When the family pet appeared wounded, many questions were asked. Pietro disavowed all responsibility. Alas, there was a witness, and Pietro's heinous deed was revealed. His mother took him by the ear and dragged him to his tiny bedroom where he slept in an oversize vegetable bin.

"How could you tell your own mother such a lie?" Beatrice said. "Do you know how I have cared for you and defended you? Have I mentioned that I was in labor for fourteen hours with you?"

"Repeatedly," Pietro said.

"You have disgraced the sign of the sonnet which is forever upon your forehead."

"I am truly sorry. I think he has distemper. He is not a desirable dog."

"I know," she said, her hand to her forehead. "I despise that animal. His face reminds me of your Uncle Luigi, about whom the less is said the better. Your father always wants to socialize with those insipid fruit-sellers. I have tried to redirect him to the fleece merchants, or the fishmongers, but he insists that a grocer must have fruit. And so we go to these people's home, and there's the dog, always the dog, jumping into my lap, soiling my frock, licking my face, begging for attention, sniffing where he should not sniff." She raised her head, eyelids flitting. "But lying is bad. You should never lie."

"I know that," he said in a quiet voice.

"I know you do. I just don't want you to be anything less than you can be. You are a good boy, Pietro."

Pietro *was* a good boy, so good it was almost impossible to be angry with him, even when he was at his most precocious. All the neighbors knew he was a good boy. As he crossed the bridge to visit his father, the other shopkeepers would remark, "There goes young Pietro. He is a good boy." The baker often slipped him day-old pastries, and when he did, he never failed to remark, "That Pietro is a good boy." The young ladies of the evening stayed clear of him, and spread the word to others in their Guild to do likewise because, they explained, "He is a good boy."

Pietro was glad to be liked and appreciated—especially since it was becoming increasingly apparent to him that he had the face of a doofus. He was one of the most popular boys in the San Frediano neighborhood, despite the fact that he had no athletic ability and tended to ramble on at considerable length about Petrarchan verse. Boys invited him on their nighttime revels. Girls giggled nervously as he passed and hinted that they would not object to strolling with him along the Arno after dark. But Pietro remained busy with his writing and his studies. Not until he was seventeen was his attention diverted elsewhere.

Pietro fell fiercely in love with Sophia Ponticelli the very day her family moved to Florence.

The time was right, hormonally speaking, for a love interest, but no one could have calculated what would happen when Pietro met Sophia. Though young, she was already a paragon of pulchritude. Her hair was as black as a moonless night, thick as a paintbrush, smooth as velvet. She had large brown eyes, long lush lashes, just a hint of freckling, and a figure the Venus de Milo would have envied.

Pietro was not the only boy enamored of her. His chums boasted of what they would do with her if they ever had the chance, which none ever did. They found it difficult to concentrate when she was nearby. Even a prominent headmaster transferred to another school. There were whispers of certain improprieties, but the truth is he simply could not focus on academic work in the presence of a beauty that transcended human experience.

To Pietro, Sophia was a goddess. So much so that, although he had a voice like an angel and was thought to be relatively good with words, he had never been able to speak to her. With her, the budding poet was tongue-tied.

And there was another problem. Sophia was the daughter of a highly successful jeweler, known as Umberto the Unctuous. Although he was not so prominent and prosperous as, say, the top-ten-ranked Florentine poets, he was sufficiently successful to ensure that Sophia's parents and Pietro's did not travel in the same social circles.

And there was one additional problem that should be mentioned. Umberto the Unctuous was the son of the Grand Inquisitor.

Which meant Sophia was the Grand Inquisitor's granddaughter.

Pietro made a point of visiting Umberto's jewelry shop every day, hoping to steal a look at the man's daughter. Instead, he saw only the father, who pursed his lips at Pietro's shabby clothes and tousled hair. Clearly, he thought about Pietro much as Pietro's mother thought of the fruit-seller's dog.

But one beautiful April day, as Pietro left the shop, he heard an angel singing.

He followed the music across the wide and crowded bridge, through the gates of the city, until he finally discovered its source at the base of the famed Campanile. As you may have surmised, the singer was Sophia.

Unfortunately, Pietro remained unable to speak to her, and after several minutes of staring from this quiet lad with the doofus face, she felt uncomfortable.

"Did you want something?" she inquired.

"W-W-W-Was t-t-t-that…" he stuttered. "Y-Y-Y-Y-You…?"

"Yes. Don't we attend school together?"

He nodded.

"Aren't you the one they say bears the sign of the sonnet?"

Again he nodded.

"And aren't you the one they say has a voice like an angel?"

He struggled mightily, trying to force words to his lips. "I-I-I-I-" He closed his eyes, swallowed. "I m-m-m-maaaaay..." He tapped his toes, thrust his hands into his pockets. He would not let this moment pass. "I m-may," he began again, slowly and steadily, "have a voice *like* an angel. But you have the voice *of* an angel."

She smiled, not because she had been flattered, but because she adored men who knew how to use words well. In her experience, men with money and muscles were fairly commonplace, but men with words were few and far between.

She reached out. "Will you walk with me?"

He could not say no. He could not say anything at all.

They strolled along the banks of the Arno for close to an hour, until the orange sun set behind the glorious Florentine skyline and they both knew her father would be wondering where she was. Pietro needed that much time to recover his voice. But when at last he did, he did not hesitate to use it.

"I have not lived long," he said, "but so long as I can remember, I have dreamed of marrying a woman with the voice of an angel."

"That is a strange and wonderful coincidence," she replied. "Because I have always dreamed of marrying a poet."

They joined hands, pledged themselves to one another before the eyes of God, and considered themselves engaged from that day forward.

This was the turning point in Pietro's life. He had always aspired to becoming a poet. But with these few precious words from Sophia, his goal became more than a personal aspiration. It became a necessity. He knew Sophia's father would never consent to marry her to the son of a vegetable merchant, but he could hardly resist the troth of a Florentine poet. Once he completed his studies, Pietro could have everything that mattered to him, everything he had ever wanted. As soon as he graduated from the Academy and joined the Guild, Sophia would be his.

Or so he believed.

Five

T he day Pietro turned eighteen, his parents took him to the Academy of Florentine Poetical Arts. They both accompanied him for several reasons. Because of the immersive nature of the instruction, all students were required to live in residence, so his parents would not see Pietro often until he completed the four-year program. They were also concerned that after the passage of so much time, the High Council might not recall its promise of admission. Sal was more cordial and businesslike, but Beatrice knew how to get a job done.

Both parents were startled when the Grand Inquisitor himself greeted them at the door. He appeared to have aged twelve years in six, as so often happens to those of a sour temperament, but he was still quick and spry and imminently dangerous.

"What brings you good people to the Academy?" he asked, invisible hands clasped.

"We are bringing our son so he may begin his studies," Sal explained.

"Splendid. Has he filed an application?"

"We were told that he did not need to make an application."

"That would be quite irregular. Who said such a thing?"

"The leader of the High Council," Beatrice replied.

"But—" The Inquisitor glanced at Pietro, who by the age of eighteen had filled out nicely and was almost a foot taller than the older man. "Could this possibly be young Pietro? The boy who had such sport with me when he was but twelve years of age?"

Having seen the Inquisitor both openly hostile and now, pretending to be friendly, Pietro preferred the former. "It is. I turn eighteen today, and so I have come as invited."

"I see." The Inquisitor smiled, but he did not move out of the way.

"Is there anything more that needs be done?" Beatrice asked. "Surely the word of the leader of the High Council is inviolate."

"Yes."

"Has anyone posed an objection to Pietro's admission?"

"No, of course not. But the Academy is not cheap. The fees might be a strain for an impecunious greengrocer."

"Not to worry," Sal said, with no small amount of pride. "The fees will be paid, whatever the cost. That is no obstacle to his studies."

"And what of you?" the Inquisitor said, turning his attention to Beatrice. "Can you perhaps think of some reason why your son should not be cloistered away for four years, far from the tender breast of the woman who raised him?"

"No, none," Beatrice replied. "He's a good boy, and with the exception of one incident when he was thirteen, he has a spotless character."

"Oh my. What happened when he was thirteen?"

She shrugged. "Boys will be boys."

The Inquisitor turned his attention to Pietro. "And what of you, young man? Is this what you want to do?"

"It is," Pietro answered. "I want it very much."

The Inquisitor's lips curled in a slow and disturbing fashion. "And would that be for yourself? Or for my granddaughter?"

Pietro felt his heart slip out of his chest. He knew. *He knew!*

"Are you aware that your son has been carrying on with a young woman above his station?"

Beatrice did not hesitate. "I do not believe any woman is above my son's station."

"Are you aware that he seeks this position not out of devotion to the poetical arts but so that he may impress a girl?"

Pietro's tongue thickened. "I want this for myself," he said, which was true, in a way. "It is what I have always wanted."

"Are you sure, boy?" As before, the Inquisitor leaned in much too close for Pietro's comfort. "Because if it is not so, if your devotion to poetry is not sincere, you will never graduate."

"I am sure," Pietro said firmly.

"Very well." The Inquisitor swept his robe back in a dramatic fashion that recalled the Grim Reaper. "Please enter our hallowed domain."

A FEW WORDS SHOULD BE SAID ABOUT THE RIGOROUS COURSE OF poetical instruction provided by the Academy. One might assume that, since the instructors were all poets or retired poets, they might be sensitive sorts inclined to take the class outside and spend the afternoon sniffing daisies. That would be incorrect. The instructors were without exception, to use the Italian technical term, "*cruedele bastardi.*" To put it another way, they were mean. They prided themselves on their meanness. They competed to be the meanest. They felt that they were the standard bearers for all poetry, so if they were less than rigorous, every reader on earth might suffer the consequences.

The instructors employed what was known as the Socratic Method, which basically meant they asked a lot of questions without providing any answers. Students were required to stand and recite, and woe betide the student who was unprepared. The first year they learned the various poetical forms, the couplet and the clerihew, the sestina and the sonnet and hundreds of others. The second year focused on the rhetorical literary devices a poet might employ, hundreds of them, from asyndeton to zeugma. During the third year they acquired expertise in rhythm and meter, iambs and triambs, scansion and syllabary. The final year, said by some to be the hardest of all, focused on theme, creating a worldview, employing ambiguity and abstraction to enhance metaphor and imagery.

Pietro did well in school. Despite the harshness of his instructors, and the intimidating suspicion that some were hoping he would fail—he did not. He kept up with his reading and turned in all his assignments. He whipped through the tests at blistering speed. He simply smiled when the instructors called him "the Bard" or "Maestro" or "the Anointed One." He persevered. When the first year came to an end, he turned in his completed exam before the instructor had finished handing them all out. He made a perfect score.

During his second year, Pietro's meanest instructor was Ferdinand Limoncello. (The Grand Inquisitor did not teach a class because he was an administrator, which might go far in explaining his temperament.) Limoncello made it his personal mission to bring down the Anointed One. Every class, he called on Pietro first and often spent half the period taking him through what came to be known as the Lightning Round of Rhetoric.

"Pietro, describe and distinguish parataxis and hypotaxis."

Pietro stood and delivered. "Parataxis is the use of successive independent clauses with coordinating conjunctions or no conjunctions at all. Hypotaxis is the use of subordination to show the relationship between the clauses. Hence, it is the opposite of parataxis."

"Provide an example of parallelism."

"Ask not what poetry can do for you; ask what you can do for poetry."

When at last, on the final day of his second year, Pietro again completed the Lightning Round without missing a question, his fellow students responded with rousing applause. Even Limoncello joined in. Pietro advanced to the next level.

The final exam at the end of the third year was familiarly known as the *"Non Vincere,"* or to put it in the vernacular, the No-Win Poetry Scenario. Although they all tried their best, no student had ever conquered it. There was a reason. Although the students did not know this—it was a tightly guarded secret—the assignment had no solution. The *Non Vincere* was not designed to test knowledge or skill. It was a test of humility, a characteristic considered essential to the first-rate poet. The instructors wished to see, not what the student knew, but how he would conduct himself in the face of the inevitable defeats that arise in every poet's life.

This oral examination was given by an instructor so mean no one even knew his name. They simply called him *"Crudele Bastardo."* To his face.

He liked it.

Pietro stood at the front of the classroom. Crudele removed the test question from a sealed envelope. "Give us four lines of iambic pentameter in which you provide both a syllogism and an enthymeme. You have two minutes."

Pietro worked feverishly, but when the time elapsed, he had not solved the puzzle. "It is impossible," he complained. "Enthymeme is by definition a syllogism missing a premise or conclusion. But without that step, there is no syllogism. With it, there is no enthymeme."

"I see you are not up to the task," Crudele said gravely. "The intricacies of the rhetorical arts still elude you. Return to your room and contemplate whether you would not be better suited to another profession, such as the selling of turnips."

The pedagogical strategy was that the student would spend the evening wrestling with self-doubt. Those who succumbed to it would depart, leaving those who had humbly accepted their limitations but remained determined to soldier on.

Pietro spent the evening in a different manner.

The next morning, he asked if he could take the *Non Vincere* again.

Permission was granted. The evaluating committee reassembled. Once again, Crudele acted as proctor. He removed the test question from a sealed envelope. "Give us four lines of iambic pentameter in which you provide both a syllogism and enumeratio. You have two minutes."

"That's easy enough," Pietro said, yawning. "I love her voice, her sweet angelic voice/I love her eyes, her hair, her face, her lips/Therefore I must love her and always shall."

"Objection," the Grand Inquisitor said, rising in the gallery. "That was not the assignment. You were supposed to provide a syllogism and an enthymeme."

"No," Pietro corrected, "that was yesterday. Today he asked for enumeratio."

"It was supposed to be enthymeme!" the Inquisitor insisted. "You must have gotten into my office. You must've changed the question!"

A hush fell over the assemblage.

"I want an enthymeme!" the Inquisitor shouted. "I want it now!"

"An enthymeme," Pietro said calmly, "is defined by omission. In this case, what I have omitted is that which made the assignment impossible. Is that not what all great poets do? Omit that which is not beauty or truth, and dwell on that which is?"

The evaluating committee applauded.

Despite the Inquisitor's protestations, and his frequent use of the unkind word "cheating," Pietro passed to the fourth year. With a commendation for grace under pressure.

At this point, Pietro appeared to be on an unstoppable course toward graduation. He had outperformed every student who had come before him. Those in the inner circles already made plans to attend his first recital at the Christmas Eve service after he graduated. None of his instructors doubted that he would finish his final year. And neither did Pietro. He could feel the diploma in his hand. He could feel Sophia's lips brushing against his. He could see them joined for all time, forever man and wife.

He could not possibly know the unforeseen and shattering events that soon would follow.

Six

I n truth, the Academy was mostly easy for Pietro. Memorizing forms and rhetorical devices was no great challenge for him. He had withstood far more intensive testing when he was twelve. Meter was in his blood, in the first step he took and every step thereafter. And although he had to work a little harder at theme, he was a bright and intuitive young man. He enjoyed analyzing the words of the top-flight poets to uncover their underlying meanings.

Despite the fact that he outshone them, Pietro enjoyed the friendship of almost all the other students at the Academy. The other boys (women would not be admitted to the Academy until 1920) admired and respected Pietro. They spent many a late night together, sipping porto and discussing matters great and small. Pietro tended not to wax on about poetry. He spoke almost exclusively of Sophia.

"If you could see her, my friends, if you could hear her voice—"

"Stop speaking so much about Sophia!" This came from his best friend at the Academy, a vintner's son christened Paolo, but affectionately known by his fellow academicians as "the Ass." This reflected not on his personality but his tendency to overuse assonance. "We have heard this all before. Sophia is the moon and the pool and the food—"

"Well, she is," Pietro replied.

"And Sophia is the proud round shroud that flies in high white—"

"You're being an Ass again," Pietro said.

"My father says a poet should forego fondness for females."

"Advice he did not take himself, apparently."

"My father says the same thing," said Georgio, a tailor's son. "According to him, a poet must have his head and heart focused on his work, not forever trying to figure out what he has done wrong this time."

"The right woman will be an inspiration, not a hindrance. That is what it means to be a muse."

"You have your head in the clouds, Pietro."

"If you had met her, Georgio, even if only for a day, an hour, a mere moment—you would feel as I do."

"Then I hope I never meet her."

Because opportunities to leave the compound were rare, none of Pietro's friends had ever seen Sophia. He himself was lucky if he saw her once a season. But each time they reunited, his ardor and devotion multiplied many times over.

The spring before he took his final examination, Pietro and Sophia met at a shady spot outside the city but still close enough to the Arno that they could feel the breeze off the water and hear the ripple and flow as it cascaded past them. Pietro spread a blanket and they had a picnic, though one composed entirely of vegetables his father had not been able to sell the previous day.

"Did you receive my letter?" Pietro asked after they finished eating. The sun was no longer at its apex and it seemed there was no one in the entire universe but the two of them. "Sometimes it's hard to slip correspondence out. They wish us to be isolated from the world of secular desires, but the scullery maid will make deliveries for a small fee. When the Grand Inquisitor is not looking."

"I did receive your note," Sophia said, a teasing smile playing on her face.

"And…was it pleasing?" He could not be more clearly fishing if he had strolled into the stream in waders.

"The letter was well-composed. I would expect nothing less from you." She leaned toward him and lightly touched his hand. "The poem you included was exquisite."

"It was a combination of great themes wrought in classic sonnet mode."

"I thought them the most beautiful words I have ever read."

"They had to be."

"And why is that?"

"Because they were for you."

She took his hand and held it for many moments before she shared her secret. "I have written a song."

"That's wonderful! May I hear it?"

"It will be familiar to you." She paused. "I have set your poem to music."

And then she sang it for him. At first, hearing his words embarrassed him. What before had seemed poetic and lovely now seemed clumsy and unworthy. But after a few moments, he stopped thinking about himself and started focusing on the music. Her voice, as always, captured his heart and transported him. Her voice could have made a bill of sale beautiful. But something was happening that was undeniably…unique. The merger of his words and her music produced a composition greater than the sum of the two components. They coupled with such precision that it seemed as if they had been created for one another, as if they were meant to be joined and only became whole once they were united. And would remain so forever.

Pietro's heart filled with such joy that he did not know what to say. Tears came unbidden. He worried she would think him weak. Those worries were brushed aside when she wiped his tears with her tender fingers. They peered deeply into one another's eyes, and although no words were spoken, they both knew what had occurred.

The marriage had taken place before the marriage could take place.

Night fell before either spoke again.

"There is but one obstacle to our happiness," Sophia said quietly.

"I know. I will pass the final exam."

"Not that. My father wishes me to marry Paolo, the vintner's son."

"He wants you to wed the Ass?"

"He will outgrow his youthful indulgences."

"Why marry him? I will be a poet soon."

"But so will Paolo. And his family is wealthy. And Grandfather does not have a problem with Paolo as he does with you. I believe he has been pressuring my father. Trying to force me to wed before you graduate. Oh, Pietro, why does he hate you so?"

"The Inquisitor started despising me long ago. And every success I have seems to make it worse." He squeezed her hand tightly. "You cannot marry Paolo."

"I don't want to. But you know how my father is. Grandfather still manipulates him as if he were a little boy. And if Father arranges a marriage, I am duty-bound to comply."

"Find an excuse. Feign an illness."

"I will do what I can. Surely I can put him off long enough for you to graduate. But I cannot put him off forever. You must become a poet. Otherwise, we will have no chance to be together."

"Sophia—I am the words. You are the music. We are meant to be together."

"If it is meant to be—then it will be." Their eyes locked and remained locked as if each was afraid that if they looked away, even for a moment, the other might disappear like the morning dew.

Seven

"Very sentimental," I commented, while Giannotti stretched his legs. "But completely unrealistic."

"You speak like one who has not found happiness in love," Giannotti replied.

"Don't start. You probably overheard me mentioning that I broke up with my girlfriend before I came to Florence. But even if I hadn't, this story would still be over-the-top."

"That is the common attitude of one who has not yet been so fortunate as to find the one with whom he is meant to share a life."

"But Pietro found Sophia, they're perfect for each other, he's going to marry her and live happily ever after, etc., etc. Right?"

Giannotti exhaled heavily. "I am afraid this story is about to take a dark turn, my friend. I will require fortification." He raised a hand. "Chiara, Frangelica, please."

She appeared almost immediately with a drink for him and more hot chocolate for me. "You two have been talking for some time."

"I am telling him the story of Pietro Begnini, Florence's greatest poet."

"Ah. So wonderful. And yet so tragic."

"Tragic?" I said. "What's the tragic?"

"Soon you will know." Giannotti downed his drink. "And now, even though it gives me great pain to do so, I shall continue."

WHEN THE DAY FOR THE FINAL EXAM ARRIVED, EVEN PIETRO FELT anxious. The exam was different for each student, uniquely tailored to test both his strengths and his weaknesses. That concerned Pietro greatly. True, he had not struggled with any of the examinations thus far, unless you counted his temporary failure to conquer the third-year examination that had no solution. His friends assured him no one was better equipped to face whatever challenge the Board of Examiners chose to give him. Even his professors, always reluctant to provide their students encouragement, expressed their certainty that Pietro had nothing to worry about.

But Pietro worried nonetheless, perhaps for the first time in his life. So much depended upon this. Not only his parents' hopes, not only his personal aspirations, but his future happiness with the woman who was his other half—all hung in the balance.

The final took place in the Examination Chamber, a dark, windowless, circular room. Spectators from the Academy were allowed to watch. Normally the exams were sparsely attended as they were of no great interest to anyone other than the student being examined. But Pietro's exam was attended by virtually everyone in the Academy, staff and student alike, all curious to see the greatest of students meet his greatest challenge.

The circular room was equipped with two black leather chairs, one for the student, one for the questioner. The exam itself was kept in a hermetically sealed box, only opened after the exam began. A string quartet played urgent music, heightening the tension. The stage was dark but for the light of a single torch which burned directly into the eyes of the student. Everyone else was invisible.

Pietro's knees weakened as he walked toward the spotlight. He slid into his chair, taking care not to stumble along the way. His mouth felt dry and his throat hurt. He could hear the shuffling of feet, the sounds of all the people gathered in the circular rows around and above him. In his first year, they had discussed the concept of foreshadowing and he had written about it extensively. But this was the first time he had personally experienced it.

He closed his eyes and took several deep breaths, slowly releasing them. Calm, he told himself. Calm.

He opened his eyes.

The Grand Inquisitor sat opposite him.

Pietro almost jumped out of his chair.

A thin smile crept across the Inquisitor's face. "I assume you have no objection to having me as your examiner, boy?"

Pietro knew objecting would serve no purpose. "That is your right."

A hush fell across the gallery. The Inquisitor's feelings about Pietro were well known.

"Then we shall begin."

The music started, an ominous, repetitive passage with pizzicato strings that teetered forever on the cusp of resolution, never quite finding it. Sudden bursts of sweeping violin glissandi quickened Pietro's pulse.

The Inquisitor opened the box.

Pietro noticed that he barely glanced at the parchment inside. He already knew what the questions would be.

"The examination has three parts," the Inquisitor announced. "In each of the first two rounds, you must accumulate 200 points; in the third, 400. You will need 800 points to pass. In each part, you may select the most challenging question for all 200 points, or two lesser challenges for 100. For the format of your responses, you may choose between the paradelle and the rhymed couplet."

"I'll take Rhymed Couplets for 200," Pietro replied.

"As you wish. Please remember that you must phrase your response in the form of a couplet."

Pietro heard whispering from the gallery. He knew what they were thinking. He was supposed to be the greatest student in the history of the Academy—and they were asking him to compose couplets? Two rhymed lines? The simplest of assignments? Pietro didn't care. He was relieved to know the task was something he could handle.

"First," the Inquisitor began, "compose a couplet that employs self-reflection and paradox with the theme of poetry itself."

Pietro thought several moments before answering. Could this be some sort of trick? He knew the Inquisitor did not want him to graduate. But this question was simple. Most of the questions he had received at the hands of Crudele required more art.

Pietro cleared his throat. "I think that I shall never see/A poem with metonymy."

The audience burst into applause. The Inquisitor's expression remained unchanged. His placid countenance was supremely disturbing.

"The second challenge of the examination," the Inquisitor continued, "is to form a pangrammatical couplet. One in which every letter of the alphabet is used at least once. On the theme of weather."

A gasp came from the gallery. This was something a poet might be able to produce with considerable effort and revision over time, but on the spot? With a time limit? It seemed impossible—

—to the person who gasped. But he was a night janitor who did not know Pietro. He had only entered the examining room to empty the spittoons. Everyone else knew Pietro could accomplish this assignment standing on his head.

"Oh, I forgot one detail," the Inquisitor added. "Your response must be composed in thirty-five letters or less."

At *that* point, everyone gasped. This task would be impossible for most students even with prior planning. Some of the letters in the alphabet appear so infrequently in Italian that composing any holalphabetic sentence would be difficult. But to include them all in a couplet of thirty-five letters or fewer? That allowed the duplication of so few letters as to make the assignment virtually inconceivable?

Pietro did it in thirty-one.

"Quick zephyrs blow," he began, rearranging the letters in his head. "Vexing daft Jim so."

The audience cheered. Everyone present realized they had just witnessed A Moment. Something that would be talked of for generations to come. And they would always have the privilege of saying, perhaps casually in passing, "I was there." No one has ever commented upon Judy Garland's historic Carnegie Hall concert without some elderly soul remarking, "I was there." Woodstock in 1969? "I was there." So many have said this that one wonders how so many people fit on that small farm. So it was with this Moment, because for decades hundreds of Florentines would claim to be among the blessed few who witnessed Pietro creating a pangrammatical couplet in his head.

"That brings us to the final part of the examination," the Inquisitor said, his expression still tranquil and unperturbed. "With one couplet, you may obtain the remaining 400 points you need to graduate." He paused. "Here is your topic. Provide one completely original metaphor."

A hush fell over the examining room. Even the music stopped.

Pietro stared into space, glassy-eyed.

"You have two minutes." The Inquisitor turned over a sandglass. "Do you understand the assignment?"

"I—I understand."

"Good. Let me know when you are prepared to respond."

Pietro looked like a child lost on the piazza on Sunday morning. "Completely original?"

"Just so, anointed bard. Tell us something we have not heard before. Ever."

"B-But—"

"Surely you agree that a poet should make a unique contribution to the arts?"

Pietro stared straight ahead.

"Surely you realize there is more to poetry than technique? More to the creation of art than a knowledge of rhetorical devices and syntax and scansion?"

"Y-Yes."

"Then make your contribution now. Give us a completely original metaphor. All you need is one. One little metaphor and you graduate with honors."

The examining room was so quiet spectators could hear Pietro swallow. They could see each bead of sweat as it dripped from his temples. Most of those in the gallery adored Pietro, so his pain was their pain, felt just as intensely as if they themselves had been sitting in the black leather chair. Some murmured words of encouragement to him under their breath. Some clenched their rosaries and said a silent prayer.

"You have only thirty seconds remaining," the Inquisitor said. "What are you waiting for?"

Pietro cleared his throat. "My, um, my love is like—"

The Inquisitor shook his head.

"The orange glow of the sun—"

"No."

"Your face is a flower that—"

"I don't think so." The Inquisitor glanced at the sandglass. "Ten seconds."

The spectators gaped in horror, feeling that they were now witnesses, not to A Moment but to A Tragedy. Worse, An Execution. They had been so assured of Pietro's technical skills that they did not consider originality. No one did but the Inquisitor, who had lain awake nights devising a test that would prevent Pietro from graduating.

"I'm so sorry," the Inquisitor said gravely. "Your time has expired. You have failed the test. You will not graduate. You will not be permitted to join the Guild. You should gather your meager belongings and leave at once."

"B-But—"

"There is nothing more to say. Your time here was a mistake, as I have maintained from the outset, and now it is over. If you are not gone in fifteen minutes, your belongings will be cast to the street."

Pietro sat dumbstruck. He felt riveted to the chair, unwilling or unable to move. Eternal happiness had dangled within his grasp. And now, in the space of a second, the dream had been crushed. There would be no second chance. No appeal. No alternate route. He would never be a poet. And that meant—

The Inquisitor left and the audience dispersed. Pietro remained in the chair. Some of his friends tried to comfort him, but to no avail.

"There are other occupations than poetry," Georgio said. "Perhaps you could enter politics."

"I hear they are hiring at the Walled Market," suggested another.

"You could move to Venice. Become a gondolier."

And that was when, in the midst of all the friends gathered around—

He realized Paolo was not among them.

Pietro burst out of his chair and raced through the assemblage, running at top speed for the front door. He did not stop to collect his belongings. He cared nothing for belongings. He cared only for the girl with the voice of an angel. He must find her.

Before it was too late.

Eight

Pietro sprinted through the streets of Florence, dodging fruit carts and caravans. Perhaps he could reach Sophia before the bad news did. He would urge her to flee with him, to run away, elope. They could run far from this accursed town and its Academy. They did not need poetry to be happy. They had each other. He would scrub the seal of the sonnet off his forehead. He would—

He careened into the front door of Sophia's home with such speed that he did not need to knock. His body announced his arrival. A few seconds later, the elderly servant Carmine opened the door.

"Master Pietro," he said in a sonorous tone. "So grieved to hear of your disappointment."

"You already know?"

"Word travels quickly in Florence, where we take our poetry very seriously."

"May I speak to Sophia?"

"I'm afraid that is not possible."

Pietro tried to force his way through the door, but the servant blocked his path.

"I don't care what your orders are. I have to see her."

"You misapprehend my statement, Master Pietro." In fact, Carmine had once dreamed of being a poet himself. Consequently, he was more sympathetic to Pietro's quest than he could openly express. "The young mistress is not at home."

"Where is she?"

"I cannot say for certain. She left with Master Paolo."

"I don't believe it."

"He arrived approximately five seconds after you failed your test. Word travels so quickly here in Florence, where—"

"But Sophia would never go with him."

"I believe she had little choice. Her father was quite forceful. When her hopes with you were dashed, he compelled her to accept Paolo's hand."

"No." Pietro gripped the man by the shoulders. "Where have they gone?"

"I believe she is at Master Paolo's home. And by this time," he added with evident regret, "they are surely joined as husband and wife."

"WAIT A MINUTE," I PROTESTED. "THAT'S NOT HOW THE STORY goes."

Giannotti raised an eyebrow. "I am rather certain that it is."

"Look, I've been writing all my life. I know how stories work. There are only five plots. And this isn't one of them. This entire narrative has been structured toward a climax in which Pietro becomes a successful poet and marries Sophia and learns valuable life lessons, yadda yadda yadda."

"If only it were so. But that is not what happened."

"It is!" Out the corner of my eye, I saw Giannotti give Chiara a look I found difficult to interpret.

"I believe I see the problem now," Giannotti said. "You are an artist. You are accustomed to creating work as best suits your artistic purposes. So when you can't make things go as you wish, you become frustrated."

"Spare me the amateur psychology."

"I need no degree to observe that you are sitting on that loveseat alone."

I folded my arms across my chest. "What has that got to do with anything? I just don't like to see you messing up your story."

A small smile played on the proprietor's lips. "Perhaps you should let me continue."

PIETRO WAS CONFUSED, DRAINED, AND WEAK AT THE KNEES, BUT HE nonetheless raced to Paolo's home with impressive speed. He pounded on the door, shouting at the top of his lungs. Many neighbors poked their heads out, but no one opened the door. Pietro did not relent. After this had gone on for more than an hour, Pietro's mother arrived (one of the neighbors informed her that her boy was making a spectacle of himself) and tapped him on the shoulder.

"No one is home," Beatrice said. "The newlyweds are on their honeymoon."

"She would not do that. Not without speaking to me first."

"She was not given options. Sophia is a dutiful, if headstrong child. Once you were out of the running, there was nothing she could do to resist her father's wishes."

"How can you be sure?"

"I saw the priest enter Paolo's home. Through the window, I watched him perform the ceremony. I saw Paolo and Sophia depart together, hand in hand."

"It cannot be."

"I'm afraid it is. The best path for you now is to get on with your life."

"I have lost both my loves, Sophia and the dream of being a poet. I have no life."

Beatrice poked him in the soft spot between his clavicle and arm. "Is that how I raised you? To be a whiner? No. I raised you to be a good boy, and you have been mostly, except for that one time when you were thirteen about which the less said the better. Listen to me, Pietro. When a window closes, a door opens."

"I shall not pass through it. There is nothing left that has any meaning for me."

Beatrice tried to persuade her son to come home, but he refused. He went back to Sophia's house, but her father refused to open the door, shouting that Sophia was married now so Pietro could have no contact with her, and good riddance. Pietro returned to Paolo's house, and there he sat, waiting for his love to return. Cold winds blew, but he waited. The winter snows fell, but he waited. Days turned into weeks, but he waited.

From time to time, the locals would bring him water, scraps of food. When the chill set in, the neighborhood association allowed him to build a small fire to warm himself. Most people were kind because in Pietro's eyes they saw the kind of love they remembered once having, or wished they had now, and besides, how can you not feel kindly toward such a good boy at his darkest moment?

With spring came the fading of the frost and the return of green to the Tuscan hills surrounding Florence. And eventually, spring brought back Paolo as well.

The former friend tried to rush past, but Pietro grabbed his arm and held him fast. Pietro had not shaved in weeks. He was dirty and disheveled. His voice creaked from lack of use. Still, he managed to grind out words. "Where...is...Sophia?"

"In our bed," Paolo said pointedly.

"I must...speak to her."

"That is impossible. And you need a bath."

"If she tells me she does not want me, I will go."

"You will go now, because this is my property and I wish it.

And you will not speak to Sophia, because she is now my property, too, and I forbid it."

"Just one minute with her."

"No. You will never speak to her again. Do you understand me?"

Pietro's teeth clenched. "You are jealous of me because you know I am a better poet."

"Except actually," Paolo said, "you're not a poet at all, are you? I'm sorry events have turned out as they did, but I've won and you've lost. The contest is over."

"I must speak to Sophia."

"If you attempt it, I will file charges against you. And if you do not leave my property, I will have you arrested as a vagrant." He pushed Pietro away. "It's my understanding that you are currently without employment."

His former friend's words pierced him like a broadsword. Pietro had been so desperate to see Sophia he had thought little about what he might say when they met. She had fallen in love with a poet, a man who could supply words for her music. But he had lost the right to use words. Now he could be nothing to her.

Unless he regained the status he had lost.

"Fine," Pietro swore. "If the Poets' Guild will not have me, I will start a rival organization of my own."

He returned to his parents' home and cleaned himself up. Then he set to work on his new plan. He founded what he called the League of Poets. He knew there were others who had been spurned by the Guild or burned by the Academy. He would unite them. In the dark of night, he swore an oath by the moon and heaven itself, raising his fist into the air.

"I swear by Erato, the muse of the love poem, that my voice will not be suppressed. I bear the seal of the sonnet. And I shall rise again!"

Alas, making oaths is much simpler than creating an organization of poets, particularly in Florence, where they take their poetry very seriously. Although there were many with grudges against the closed-shop hegemony of the Guild-Academy trust, they were hesitant to do anything to offend the status quo. Florence had a long-standing institutional opposition to scab poets. He could not build a league without sponsorship, but he could not attract a sponsor without poets.

Since he could not attract the disaffected, he scoured the seventeen-year-olds of Florence for untainted candidates. But his first-draft pick ended up signing with the Academy, as did his second, third, and fourth, lured by lucrative signing contracts and shiny carriages. The Inquisitor, it seemed, was aware of his activities and constantly worked behind the scenes to prevent him from succeeding.

Pietro took his cause to the streets, standing on a vegetable box in the piazza outside the Duomo.

"Listen to me, people of Florence. Poetry is art! No one can own art. It is not a commodity to be bought and sold. It belongs to everyone. Let us throw off the shackles of Guild despotism. Let us set the words free!"

After a time, Pietro attracted some attention. By the end of the week, a respectable crowd gathered around his box, listening attentively and at times even offering rumbles of support.

That was when the Inquisitor made an appearance.

"This all sounds like the sour grapes ranting of a would-be poet who proved not up to the task," the Inquisitor said in a placid voice that nonetheless resonated throughout the piazza.

"And you sound like one who wants to control poetry rather than nurture it," Pietro replied.

The Inquisitor let out a small chuckle. "My dear boy, would you let chaos reign? Poetry is too important to be left to amateurs. It belongs precisely where it is, in the hands of trained professionals, those who have read and studied and know what they are about when they set pen to parchment."

"No one owns poetry!" Pietro shouted back.

"I do not say we should own it. I only say we should instruct those who would use it. Would you let any untrained vegetable salesman become a surgeon? Of course not. Why should it be any different for something so much more important to our spiritual wellbeing? Do we not want only the most qualified to wield the scalpel of words?"

"Poetry is not surgery!"

"Of course not. I was employing a metaphor. An original metaphor. So I am not surprised that you failed to grasp it."

Pietro tried to frame a response, but once again, in the presence of this man, words abandoned him. The crowd dispersed. He was alone.

Pietro plunged into despondency. For weeks he did nothing but sit in the basement of his parents' home chucking onions into a vegetable bin. His beard grew longer. He ate nothing but cheese pasta. He forgot to change his clothes. He forgot to bathe. He tried to write poetry, but found himself writing, *"Ti amo, Sophia,"* over and over again. After penning the same words fourteen-thousand six-hundred and twenty-two times, his mother took away his vellum. So he wrote it on the walls. She hung tapestries on the walls. He wrote it in the air.

His family knew his heart had been broken, twice, so they were sympathetic. But even the kindest heart will ice after someone has gone two months without changing his socks. So his father had a talk with him.

"You are a good boy," Sal began. "If you cannot be a poet, be something else."

"There is nothing else. Nothing that matters."

Sal ignored the implicit jab. "Of course there is. You could be a tinker, a tailor—let's omit beggar man and thief—doctor or lawyer or Indian caliph, which really doesn't rhyme as well as it should."

"It was probably composed by someone who couldn't pass his final examination."

Sal cleared his throat. "I, um, wondered if you might like to come to the vegetable stand with me tomorrow."

Pietro did not respond.

"I could use some help." Sal stretched his arms, cracking his knuckles. "Not as young as I used to be. Hauling those potatoes around gets tiring."

Still no answer.

"And if you wanted to watch the stand on occasion, that would be all right. Get tired of standing on my feet all day."

Pietro looked up slowly, his eyes emerging from the darkness. "I am not going into the vegetable business."

Sal shrugged. "I wouldn't object to a little assistance, that's for sure. And...near as I can tell, you don't have anything else taking up your time."

Pietro sat up straight. "I am not going into the vegetable business."

"Son, I know you've had some disappointments. Tough ones. We've tried to be patient. But you're twenty-two years old. It's time you had some kind of living."

Pietro had been pushed to the brink of despair and now, sadly, his frustration got the better of him. "Do you think I intend to spend the rest of my life sorting produce? I'm an educated man. I bear the sign of the sonnet! I won't be reduced to...to peddling potatoes!"

Sal said nothing.

Pietro threw himself onto the floor. "Leave me alone."

His father left the room.

When his mother brought her son his gruel the next morning —he was gone. He had disappeared. No one knew where he had gone. Everyone feared the worst.

He was not seen again in Florence for eighteen years.

Nine

"This is where my story becomes more difficult," Giannotti announced. The night was so dark that his head was a barely visible silhouette against the blue-black sky.

"Because you're making it up as you go along?" I asked.

"Don't be cynical. This is history, but as you may know, sometimes there is more than one history. And at other times, none at all."

"Because you're making it up as you go along."

"What I am trying to explain is that for hundreds of years after Pietro's disappearance, no one knew where he went after he left Florence."

"No one?"

"No one."

"For eighteen years?"

"There is some precedent for this sort of thing. For those who know the history of Florence's greatest poet, this time is a blank chapter titled '*Pietro: The Missing Years.*'"

"You're telling me that the greatest poet in the history of a city that takes its poetry very seriously disappeared for eighteen years and no one knew where he was?"

"No one."

"I went off for a weekend once with this co-ed from Tucson, and before we got back, everybody knew where we'd been."

"In Pietro's time, there was no social networking. No surveillance. No fingerprints. No DNA. Witness Martin Guerre. Not only vanished, but replaced. In this era, if a man wanted to disappear, he could disappear."

"Do you know where Pietro went when he disappeared?"

Giannotti eased into his chair, steepling his fingers at eye level. "My grandfather was obsessed with Pietro Begnini."

"Seems to run in the family."

"He spent thousands of liras, and many years of his life, investigating the truth behind the missing years."

"Did he learn anything?"

"Not for decades. Despite his concerted efforts and dozens of paid investigators. And then, in the last days of the millennium, he uncovered a handwritten journal hidden in a wine vat in an obscure Tuscan village."

"Why would anyone put a journal in a wine vat?"

"To keep it safe, my friend."

"And very damp, I would think."

"It was protected by an airtight goatskin wrapping."

"Why put it there at all?"

"Because, although the author was sworn to secrecy during his lifetime, he did not want this story to be lost. You see, the author was a man of learning. He knew that future generations would be interested in this tale."

"I assume you know the contents of this journal."

Giannotti nodded.

"And the journal reveals Pietro's whereabouts during his missing years."

"In part."

"Then let's get on with the story."

❧

NEEDLESS TO SAY, PIETRO'S PARENTS WERE CONCERNED WHEN HE disappeared. For that matter, almost everyone in Florence was worried. Despite his setbacks in life and love, Pietro was still the good boy with the seal of the sonnet and much adored throughout the neighborhood of San Frediano. Search parties were formed. An all-night vigil lasted three weeks. Messengers and scouts were sent south to Rome and north to Venice. But no one could find any trace of the missing Pietro.

And then, one dark day, a scrap of red cloth was found in the mouth of a slain wild pig. Some said the cloth resembled a kerchief worn by Pietro. Others said it was impossible to be certain. Not surprisingly, Beatrice was the one who settled the question.

"I know this masticated cloth," she said, before hundreds of witnesses. "I cut and sewed this kerchief with my own hands. This belonged to my boy."

A gasp filled the piazza.

"Then"—the Duke of Florence said, grief plastered across his face—"there is no question?"

"None at all," she replied, showing the strength that had served her well over many trying years. "This belonged to my son, the good boy who never hurt anyone, save an obnoxious dog of no account and that only when he was thirteen and greatly provoked." She clenched the cloth in her fist. "The pig got him. My son is dead."

"AND THAT," GIANNOTTI SAID, CLAPPING HIS HANDS TOGETHER, "IS the end of my story."

"What? *What*?"

"Pietro is dead. The story is concluded."

"But—But what about all that nonsense where your grandfather finds a journal in a vat?"

"As you say, nonsense."

"You said you knew where Pietro was for eighteen years. Which suggests that he returns at the end of that time."

"He was in an unmarked grave in the foothills of Sorrento for those eighteen years. Also for five hundred and thirty-six years after that."

I leaned forward, pointing a finger. "You're messing with me!"

"Well, yes." Giannotti spread his hands expansively. "But ask yourself this. Why do you care?"

"You shouldn't start a story if you don't intend to finish it."

"You like Pietro. You empathize with him. He is a fellow poet."

"Not so far."

"And he loves deeply. With all his heart." He gave me a strange, penetrating look.

"Could we just get on with the story, Aesop? I'm worried about this pig business."

"As you wish."

Ten

It will perhaps not be too startling a plot twist if I reveal that Pietro was not in fact dead. He had encountered the wild pigs, but he was a fast runner and made it to a treetop in plenty of time. One of the younger pigs had an injured leg, and being the good boy that he was, as soon as he could do so safely, he wrapped his kerchief around the wound to staunch the bleeding. The pig eventually gnawed off the kerchief which was found in its mouth and the local authorities reached a considerably incorrect conclusion.

Pietro spent many years simply walking the earth. He had never been out of Firenze before, so there was much to see. He would work from time to time, just to make enough to get himself to the next town. If someone asked Pietro where he was going, or for what reason, he would have no answer for them. His only desires had been left far behind. Perhaps he sought an anodyne for his pain. But what Pietro learned was what so many men before and after him have learned: No matter how far you travel, there is no escaping a wounded heart.

One day, several years later, while walking along a riverbank in the North Country, Pietro encountered an older gentleman who appeared to be tinkering with some kind of mechanical device. Always curious, Pietro stopped to inquire. As it turned out, the older gentleman, who introduced himself as Leo, was fond of talk, particularly about himself and his work. He immediately saw that Pietro was a good boy, so words flowed freely. Within ten minutes, they were on first-name terms.

"I am testing a new creation," Leo explained.

"What does it do?"

"The people in the high hills need water." He was a balding gentleman overcompensating with a flowing white beard. "They tire of walking up and down the steep incline each day, never able to carry back as much water as they need."

"Has that not always been the case?"

"Indeed it has. But does that mean it must always be so?"

"This is an impossible problem."

"Are we dead?"

"Uh, no."

"Then it is not impossible. Never say the word 'impossible' to me. I take it as a challenge."

"But you cannot alter the location of the river."

The man pursed his lips. "Not today, anyway."

"So if you cannot bring the river to the hill people, the hill people must surely come to the river."

"I propose to bring water to the hill people in baked clay pipes."

"A lovely idea. But although I am no scientist, I feel certain water cannot flow uphill."

Leo removed a clay pipe, perhaps eighteen centimeters long, from his pack. The pipe opened to reveal an inner mechanism. "This valve opens and shuts at a fixed interval, allowing water to pass or to block the flow. When the valve is closed suddenly, at the end of the pipeline, it creates pressure." Leo poured water into the pipe from a small pitcher, then quickly closed the valve. The water hitting the valve changed direction with a jolt, as if hammered by an unseen force. "The pressure allows a portion of the flowing water powering the pump to be lifted to a higher elevation. In other words—water flows uphill. I propose a series of such pipes and valves routing water from the lower basin to the hill people. And thus they will obtain water. Without the necessity of descending the hill each day."

"You must be some sort of sorcerer."

"In a way. But my magic does not come from the black arts. It comes from here." He tapped the side of his head. "Are you a university man, Pietro?"

"I did attend an Academy, but it did not turn out well and I have no diploma to show for it."

"Degrees mean nothing. I have precious little formal learning myself. But I've lived my life as an autodidact."

"And that means?" Pietro hoped it was not as naughty as it sounded.

"I taught myself. Did you learn anything at this Academy?"

"Yes. I learned that I could not do the only thing I ever wanted to do, and that I could not have the only thing I ever wanted to have."

"Why not?"

"Because it is impossible."

"Are you dead?" Leo laid his hand on Pietro's shoulder. "Have you learned nothing from this demonstration? Nothing is impossible to the imaginative mind."

"I beg to differ. What I wanted is lost. There was only one path and it is permanently blocked."

"Yes, and water can only flow downhill. Or so people believed, until I demonstrated otherwise."

"But you are a great scientist—"

"I'm not a scientist at all. I'm a painter. And a sculptor, writer, code master, designer, engineer, anatomist, physician, cartographer, geographer, botanist, architect, musician, and mathematician. I like to stay busy."

"You must come from a wealthy family."

"I have virtually no family. I was born illegitimate to a notary and a peasant woman in the tiny village of Vinci. I was raised by my uncle and my grandparents. But today I travel in the best company and exchange ideas with the wisest and greatest men of our age. There are no limitations, Pietro. Except those we create for ourselves."

Leo took Pietro home with him. They worked together on the river project, and within months they had constructed a system of pipelines that delivered water reliably to more than a thousand people in Siena. Leo used the project as a test case for a larger project for the Ottoman Sultan Beyazid II of Istanbul.

During the years that followed, Leo and Pietro traveled throughout the continent and conducted many experiments together. Leo borrowed an idea from the Orient, using Kongming lanterns sent aloft on hot air for signaling. Leo believed such lanterns could be increased in size and capacity to transport cargo. They devised a large-scale balloon inflated by hot air from a portable furnace. Bags of dirt were used to control ascent and descent and tether ropes were attached to guide the balloon.

"That is simply amazing," Pietro said one day, as he observed a balloon capable of carrying sixty kilograms aloft.

"And what have you learned from this?" Leo asked.

Pietro considered a moment. "Hot air rises?"

"Nothing is impossible to the imaginative mind."

Pietro was exposed to Leo's many friends and companions. Few of them were poets, but Pietro enjoyed every learning opportunity. He painted with Leo's master, Verrocchio. Discussed politics with Machiavelli. Dined with the Medicis. Watched Michelangelo sculpt. Took art classes with Perugino and Botticelli. Debated with Thomas Aquinas. Boozed with Chaucer, who was inspired by his chance encounter with Pietro to coin the phrase: "Love is blind."

Pietro was invited to a dinner at Milan's Sforza Palace with many important men of business and politics. The only other youth at the dinner was a young woman, perhaps sixteen years of age. He did not understand her connection to the others, but he marveled at her hair, long and blonde and willowy, her pale skin, and her striking hazel eyes. When she giggled, as she frequently did, her mouth opened wide and her teeth seemed as white as a cloud.

Later that evening, being in a contemplative mood, Pietro

walked the extensive Sforza gardens alone. As he inhaled the rich scent of honeysuckle and bougainvillea, he heard a small tittering.

"Are you the poet?"

He searched the darkness. She appeared to him gradually, moving with such grace that she appeared to be floating.

"You were at dinner," he said, not knowing her name.

"As were you. I heard someone call you Leo's poet friend."

"I am not a poet," Pietro said quickly.

"I love poetry." Somehow she could laugh at the same time she talked. "Will you recite for me?"

"If you wish." He almost began, then stopped. "What shall I call you?"

"My friends call me Lucy."

"Very well, Lucy." He recited some of his friend Chaucer, but much of that he decided was too bawdy for this delicate spirit. He shared some of the ancient Florentines, some of Homer and Virgil. When he thought he had talked long enough, he finished with his countryman, Dante. But instead of *La Divina Commedia*, he favored *La Vita Nuova*.

He peered into Lucy's dancing hazel eyes. "In that book which is my memory / On the first page of the chapter that is— that is—" He stumbled, momentarily unable to remember the words.

To his great surprise, she continued for him. "On the first page of the chapter that is the day when I first met you / Appear the words, 'Here begins a new life.'"

"You know poetry," Pietro said, almost breathless.

"I told you I loved it. I believe that we are kindred spirits, Pietro, in that...and perhaps other aspects."

Pietro found his mouth dry and his tongue thick. "I...have never met a woman such as you."

"I feel the same way." With sudden impetuosity, she clasped his hand. "Take me away from here, Pietro. Let us run away together, away from estates and politics and obligations of state. Let's us revel in beauty together."

"But your family—"

"I am not even an official part of this family. My father was not married to my mother. What does it matter? He still treats me as if I were his to command. I already have been betrothed twice. To my relief, neither suitor completed the transaction. But if I remain here, it is bound to happen again. Pietro, please! Let us be lovers, running freely through the hills of Tuscany, together always."

With great heaviness of heart, Pietro removed his hand from hers. "I...cannot."

Lucy lowered her head. "You love someone else."

"Yes," he said, barely above a whisper.

"You are betrothed."

"No."

"She waits for you."

"No." He looked away, hoping to find strength by distancing himself from Lucy's beauty. "She has married another."

"Then what restrains you? Let us go! Quickly!"

"I cannot command my heart," he said. "And my heart is with another. No matter what the circumstances may be."

She gently pressed her fingers to his cheek. "Poor Pietro. Poor sad Pietro. I think you are a beautiful soul." She paused. "And I think you are destined to be a very lonely one."

Eleven

At some point, it occurred to Pietro that one possible explanation for his otherwise unfathomable inability to pass his final examination was his lack of experience. What did he know of life, after all? He had lived in Firenze all his childhood. He had spent his formative years cloistered in the Academy. Even now, as he joined Leo in his travels, his experiences never exceeded Leo's current whims.

And he never devised an original metaphor.

And so, much as he loved Leo, he decided it was time to move on. To be sure, Leo was becoming somewhat crotchetier as he aged, and Pietro tired of calming him down from the latest outrage to his sensibilities. But even more importantly, he felt that there were answers he did not have, answers to questions he did not know. And his heart ached for Sophia. His friend did not know this, as Pietro kept his pain hidden behind his sweet demeanor and doofus face. But every waking hour of every day, he pined for her. And he never relinquished his dream of being a poet. He knew most would say it was impossible.

But he was not dead.

And so at last he announced his plan to depart. As it happened, Leo was all in favor.

"There are so many wonders in the world," Leo enthused as he tinkered with his latest model, a contraption he believed might allow men to fly as birds do. "There are Spanish explorers crossing the ocean and discovering new worlds. Brunelleschi brought mathematical perspective to art. In Flanders they have a musical device which produces a sound by plucking a string when a key is pressed. In far-flung Cathay the Ming Dynasty has commissioned a work—an encyclopedia—that is said to contain all knowledge known to man. Twenty-two thousand volumes of it. The world is changing with the speed of lightning." He paused. "Except perhaps in Anglia. The greatest innovation the Scots have managed is a drink derived from water and malted barley. That's it." He let out a heavy sigh. "Not an altogether terrible effort, though."

"I want to go all those places," Pietro said. "I want to use all these great inventions. I want to see the new art and hear the new music."

"Then you should."

"But you have been so good to me. You introduced me to your world."

"Pietro. Don't get sentimental on me. Nothing binds you here. You have no wife, no children."

Pietro's eyes darted to the floor.

"You see that as a failure. You are lonely sometimes. I know. But I know this, also—loneliness is an ass. It makes us do stupid stupid things. When I was a boy—" He stopped and patted his chest. "I could tell you stories. But that is beside the point. Pietro, you can turn that ass into an asset. Your lack of ties gives you freedom. Freedom to travel with nothing but the clothes on your back and a poem in your heart. I would also recommend a florin or two in your pocket. But you see what I am saying."

"I do. But there are so many possibilities. Where should I start?"

"That is for you to decide. But I have a suggestion. You know of the efforts of Señor Gutenberg?"

"Of course I do. We had one of his Bibles at the Academy. The students were particularly fond of the Song of Solomon. And we had many volumes of poetry printed by the Gutenberg method. Mechanical press. Moveable type."

"Don't believe everything you hear. Gutenberg used a grape press to force ink onto paper. Bravo. But moveable type was invented in Venetia by hard-working Italian boys."

"I was told—"

"Bah. Look at those clumsy Bibles sometime. The letters smudged and overlapping. How could there be moveable type? He made a good ink, I give Gutenberg that. But no more." Leo shook his head. "So like the Germans. Taking credit for everything."

"Someone must have invented it."

"Look to Venetia for that, my boy. Venetia is the center of the modern publishing world. You may have your small presses here and about. But the five major publishing houses all head-quarter in that one wonderful city. The other presses do not really matter."

"I would like to see a printing press do its magical work. Putting poetry on paper."

"That would suit you well, I think. But if you go there, no matter what else you do, be sure to go nowhere near Aldus Manutius."

Pietro drew in his breath. "I have heard his name spoken at the Academy in dark whispers. I have heard him called the Devil himself."

"They did not exaggerate by much. Manutius the Devil has taken the most wonderful invention of all time—and here I mean the book—and debased it."

"How so?"

"He has invented a book—if it can be called that—not bound by boards covered with leather or calfskin or vellum. His books are simply covered by a slightly thicker stock of paper!"

"How is that a book?"

"Exactly. It is a vile imitation, a Golem. Manutius says the lower prices make the classics available to the masses. Who ever wanted them to be available to the masses? What would the masses do with them? Will we spend eternity listening to uneducated fools pontificating on the meaning of Mallory or the themes of Erasmus? He says the lighter weight enables a traveler to carry a book, or even many books, in a saddlebag and carry them on long journeys. Bah!" Leo walked to his bookshelf and ran his fingertips lovingly across the spines. "I like the feel of a book. I like the weight of it in my hands."

"And yet, the reading experience is just the same. Isn't it the text that matters, rather than the delivery system?"

"Don't bore me with your newfangled notions. That vile Venetian wants to destroy literature almost before it has begun!"

"*Tempus mutantur*," Pietro said.

"Yes, times change, but not always for the better. This is not how things were when I was young. We didn't have these newfangled telescopes or woodcuts or geometrical squares. In my day, a man had to do to an honest day's work if he wanted to succeed in the arts."

"I still would like to see a printing press in action."

"Then you must go to Venetia, my boy. Venetia!" He pulled Pietro close. "But stay away from Aldus Manutius!"

And so Pietro traveled to the Floating City, the City of Canals, the Civilization on the Archipelago. He drifted down the Grand Canal steered by a gondolier who sang the sweetest arias he had ever heard. He attended services at the Basilica Cattedrale Patriarcale di San Marco, though he was disappointed to find they had only music and liturgy and sermons—no poetry. He took tea at a table on the Piazza San Marco and watched gulls dive for bits of bread as they swooped in from the Adriatic. He watched the sun set in the sea-blue eyes of Venetian princesses. But though he looked at these women, he saw only his Sophia.

The air seemed different in Venice, as if filled with the fragrance and energy of life—plus a faint whiff of decadence.

Everywhere he saw masks and parties and gaiety, some of it of a variety that would not have been sanctioned back in San Frediano. The atmosphere both excited him and frightened him. A heady combination for an aspiring poet.

He had come to Venice hoping to see a printing press in action. Since he could not create poetry himself, he thought it might be well to watch it being printed. And since Leo had instructed him to avoid the Mephistophelean Aldus Manutius, that was of course the first place Pietro went.

The House of Manutius was the premiere printing firm in Venice, indeed, in all of Europe. His paperbound books had revolutionized the publishing world. His matching editions of the Greek and Latin classics were found in the home of every well-educated citizen, or every citizen who wanted to be thought well-educated. His house employed over thirty people. In a firm that size, Pietro thought, surely there would be a place for him.

Pietro waited three months for a meeting with Manutius. Initially, the publisher's personal secretary refused to give Pietro an audience. Finally, when Pietro identified himself as a "representative" of the Florentine Academy for the Poetical Arts, the secretary said he might be able to find some time, since Manutius hoped to add the Academy to his client list. After considerable finagling, the secretary agreed to quill-pen Pietro in for a meeting next month. But that meeting was canceled due to an ulcer, and the next was cancelled due to an ink-makers strike, so three full months passed before Pietro met Aldus Manutius face to face.

Pietro found the man perched behind his desk, shuffling papers and barking orders to an unseen assistant. Several minutes passed before he realized Pietro was present.

"Oh. Company. Great." Manutius took a codex from his desk and threw it to the floor. "I'll do the bookwork later. Can I save us both some time by speeding through the preliminaries? Yes, you have the privilege of addressing the renowned Aldus Pius Manutius the Elder, inventor of the semicolon. No, I don't donate to charity. I won't publish your grandmother's memoir, lovely though I'm sure it is. Don't bother me with short stories, essays, reflections on life, sappy stories that tug at your heart while hammering facile life lessons. Or stories about animals. I hate stories about animals."

Pietro cleared his throat. "Actually, I wasn't—"

"And no poetry. Please God, no poetry. Nothing on earth sells worse than poetry."

"That's fine," Pietro said. "None of the poets I know publish, anyway."

"Think it's beneath them, is that it? It wasn't beneath Virgil. It wasn't beneath Petrarch. But your friends probably have higher standards." He pushed up from his desk, sending parchment flying. "You're the kid from the Academy, right?"

"Well…yes."

"Can't get that stingy High Council to buy from me. They only want the expensive oversize Moroccan-leather hardcover editions. Like the poems are better somehow when the book is heavier. I tried to reason with them. Drives me crazy when I can't crack a market."

"I'm sorry, but you—"

"Look, I don't have much time. I'm just coming out of the worst punctuation crisis in the history of the industry. Probably the history of the world."

"Punctuation crisis?"

"This one has been festering since Gutenberg got the whole thing started. If it really was Gutenberg, you know what I mean? There was no uniformity in the publishing world. Everybody had their own system. You'd start reading one publisher and get used to it. Then you'd switch to a different publisher and everything changed. Periods asking questions, commas ending sentences. Madness."

"Sounds horrible."

"Chaos reigned. Crisis loomed. Till I stepped in. Set things right. Made rules, and my rules are sticking. There are now fourteen punctuation marks. That's all. Fourteen. The period—and that's how you end a sentence, no more ending with a colon, which is idiocy—question mark, exclamation point, comma—that was a toughie, had to lower the virgule for that one—dash, hyphen, parentheses, brackets, slash, apostrophe, ellipsis, quotation marks, colon, and—" He beamed. "Semicolon. That's my baby."

"That's it?"

"No hybrids. No interabang. No question comma. Be a grownup and choose already." He walked to the window and smiled as he gazed out at the stormy sea. "I quashed a revolution. How many people can say that?"

"Not many."

"Not that I haven't had crises of my own. Ever since Virgil's *Opera*, people have been whining about the pocket books. Octavos, we call them. Sounds classy, right? They're cheaper and just as good. So dry your eyes already." He turned abruptly from the window. "Do you know who invented italics?"

Pietro hesitated. "Just to hazard a guess…you?"

"Got it in one. Sure, I had Griffo down in printing work it up, but it was my idea. Slanty little letters. Very classy, don't you think?"

"I certainly do."

"But here's the secret, kid. It's a florin saver. Those italic letters can be pressed closer together. More words on a page. Less paper. Overhead reduced. Profits soar."

"I can see where that would be advantageous. But of course, publishing is not just about money."

Manutius' head tilted to one side. "Come again?"

"I know you must care deeply about literature. You've dedicated your entire life to the preservation and presentation of the works of the ancient world, rescuing them from extinction and making them available to the masses. You have increased the world's ability to appreciate the great books."

"Oh, right, the literature thing. I got you. Sure, I care about that. But you can't publish if you're losing money."

"I suppose that is true."

"You know what happened to the Library at Alexandria?"

"Burned?"

"Poof! Like a cloud of smoke. Most of Sophocles—gone! Aristophanes—gone! Aristotle on Comedy—gone! And the same thing could easily have happened again. I made sure it didn't. I put all the great works of Greek and Roman literature into plentiful, affordable editions. Now there are thousands of them all over the world. A tidal wave couldn't get rid of them all. And I've done the same for modern literature. Desiderius Erasmus—safe. Thomas Linacre—safe. My biographies have preserved the lives of the great men of history. I'm doing a public service here."

"I can see that. Most generous."

"Exactly. Just so I don't lose money in the process. Wife doesn't like that. You married?"

"No."

"My advice—don't. But enough about me. What can you do for me?"

"I...would like to see a printing press at work."

"You're a tourist?"

"I would rather be a printer."

"You? An Academy boy? Nah. I see you more as an editor."

"You mean—I would edit the work of other authors?"

"What kind of rube are you? Editors don't have time to edit. Editors take meetings. Sunup to sundown. Cover designs. Marketing plans. Sales force presentations. Handling prima-donna writers. Fortunately, most of mine are dead."

"Could I work on the poetry line?"

"Poetry? Spend all your time indulging scribes with poor grooming habits who think social awkwardness is a sign of genius? Squeeze as much work out of them as possible before they throw themselves off a bridge? That what you had in mind? No thank you."

"But—"

"This business is all about numbers." Aldus lifted the heavy codex off the floor and opened it across his desk. "Our business is at the tipping point. No more room at the inn. Barely breaking even. So I can't hire you."

"Very well. I'll—"

"Unless you can pass my test. Call it a final examination."

"I'd rather not."

"It's a simple test. I'm sure an Academy man such as yourself can handle it. You just need to come up with one thing."

"I feel as if I've taken this test before."

"Bring me one—just one—original idea."

"I *have* taken this test before."

"I'm talking publishing ideas. You want me to hire you? Fine. Bring me a new idea. If I like it, I'll hire you to make it happen. Here's the thing. I've published all the classics. Plays, epics poems, *roman-fleuves*. I've done all the histories. I've published everything that's worth publishing. I'm running out of material." He grabbed Pietro by the pockets of his waistcoat. "Bring me something new."

"And if I do?"

"Then that job is yours." He winked. "Might take you next door to see the printing press, too."

"I'm still unclear on what—"

"So you've had your time and I've got work to do. Get out of here already. Go."

Twelve

Pietro pondered Aldus's challenge for days. He'd loved his days at the Academy, until the end. He'd loved being immersed in the study of words and euphony and rhythm. He'd loved being surrounded by others who loved poetry. And then he'd been ripped out of that rarefied environment, the door slammed shut and bolted with no chance of return, all because he failed a single test.

And now he saw another failed test looming before him. Another closed door.

He was determined not to let that happen again.

He needed a new idea for a publishing line. An innovation. Something no one had done before.

Not his strong suit.

But if he'd learned anything from his time with Leo, it was that nothing was impossible. He just needed a new approach. What would that be?

If all the old stories had been told—he would find a new one. And if he could not think of one himself—he would find someone who could.

He took a boat ride to the nearby Island of San Giorgio Maggiore, a popular place for Sunday afternoon outings. He sat in a shaded spot and listened. Nothing more. Simply listened.

As people passed by, he caught snatches of conversations. Found poetry, he told himself.

"I'd be mad if he said I smelled."

"My father won't let me carry a parasol. He says it's an affectation."

"I told you I didn't want sausage. I hate sausage."

"You're overfed, overweight, and over here. Too often."

"Can you not move any faster? I'll die of old age before we get off this island."

"When you told me what you told me, I thought you meant it."

"Villon isn't fit to read Occleve's work aloud, much less imitate it."

"That woman is wearing my hat."

"I've never liked sausage. Not since the day I was born."

"I think the bird's name is Benjamin." (It is possible that Pietro misunderstood this one because the woman spoke in German.)

"There never was a Charlemagne. It's all a conspiracy concocted by the Prussians."

"No one really likes cilantro."

"Just pull the wrapper off and pretend it's mincemeat."

"The Doge didn't get the most votes. The Great Council is riddled with fraud."

"How can I tell if I'm still alive?"

"Would you please just eat the sausage?"

"Is he writing down what you just said?"

After listening to this chatter for days, Pietro realized that stories were all around him. Everyone had stories to tell. Indeed, he began to see the world as an interlocking web of stories, sometimes overlapping, sometimes overwhelming. He also came to the sad realization that many of those stories were not terribly interesting.

The law of averages suggested that one or two of them had to be noteworthy. Perhaps even original. How could he find the stories that might be of interest to Aldus Manutius?

And then it came to him. How does one find anything?

He would advertise.

On the following Sunday, Pietro obtained a permit to erect a small stand on the Piazza San Marco. Sunday was market day in Venice. He was surrounded by vendors of fruits and vegetables and sweets and tools and toys. He even spotted a few book-sellers.

He erected a placard: STORIES WANTED.

Everyone else in the market was selling something. He would be the only one who was buying.

At first, he did not see much traffic. People were unsure of his business and hesitant to approach. People looked at him out the corners of their eyes. Children pointed. But no one brought stories.

An elderly man was the first to speak to him, more than an hour after he arrived.

"You say you're selling stories?"

"No," Pietro answered politely. "Buying them."

"Buying them? For what?"

"Publication."

"You want to publish my story?"

"I couldn't say until I've heard it."

"It's quite a story, my life. You may not think much happens to a sixty-seven-year-old fisherman. You'd be surprised."

"Tell me about it."

"I was born in Verona to two of the nicest people. Never had any money. But we were happy. I remember sometimes first thing in the morning, my father would…"

And he was off. Pietro heard little that he thought would be of interest to readers, but he let the man tell the story of his life, pausing occasionally when he had another visitor. Many of the people passing through the piazza had traveled extensively and were eager to tell stories about what they had seen and heard.

"In Gaul, they tell of a sixteen-year old girl who led troops to major victories," a scholar told him.

"That seems unlikely. And the story would only appeal to other young girls, who have no purchasing power." He was learning to think like Aldus. "I do not want that story."

An amiable man with a white beard was his next visitor. "In Anglia, they tell of a dark king with a withered arm who captured and killed two young princes."

"Can't use that one," Pietro said. "Too horrific. Female readers would be unnerved by the thought of small children in danger."

He thought somewhat longer about the tale brought by a raven-tressed woman whose face was obscured by a veil. "In Wallachia, they speak of an evil prince who impaled his Ottoman enemies on pikes surrounding his castle. And he drank their blood."

"Do you say he was a vampire?"

"That is what they say in Wallachia."

"Then this is not the story for me. No one would want to read a book about a vampire."

At the end of the day, Pietro had heard little that he thought could be used by Aldus' firm. But he had heard everything there was to know about the elderly fisherman, who had sat with him the entire day and told his entire life history in detail. When night fell, Pietro prepared to leave.

"Thank you for listening," the elderly gentleman said.

"I thank you for your company," Pietro replied politely, fishing in his pocket for a florin. "You have spent so much time with me. I should pay you a little something."

The other man pushed his florin away. "I would gladly have paid you."

That was when Pietro had his epiphany.

The next day he was in Aldus' office waiting when the publisher arrived.

"I have an idea," Pietro said. "Something new. Fresh. Original. Something that hasn't been done before."

"How many times have I heard that?" Aldus brushed past him. "Okay, kid, what's the great idea?"

Pietro could barely contain his excitement. "You publish the biographies of people who are not famous. Ordinary people. People who will not make the history books but who nonetheless lived valuable lives and obtained wisdom they wish to share. We tell their stories."

Aldus laid his hand on Pietro's shoulder. "That's sweet. Really. But there's a problem with telling the life stories of ordinary people." He looked Pietro square in the eyes. "No one cares! So the publisher will lose tons of money. Get out of here and take your crazy—"

"You're missing the most important part of this," Pietro said. "We don't pay anything to publish the book. The author pays to have the book published."

"The author—" He jerked his head around. "Whaaaat?"

"The author pays you a fee to produce and distribute the book, a fee that includes generous compensation for your trouble. So it doesn't matter whether anyone buys the book. You get your money up front."

"Why would anyone do that?"

"Vanity. Pride. Or perhaps for the illusion that someone is listening to them. That they are not alone. I have heard that loneliness makes people do stupid stupid things."

Aldus sank into his chair, batting a finger against his lips. "You know—this just might work."

Pietro was hired immediately, and Aldus let him watch the printing press make an actual book. Pietro acted like a giddy child as the printers worked the moveable type, selecting letters and arranging them as they would appear on a page. The screw press cranked down to apply pressure to the paper. Once the ink stained the page, they removed the undertable and started over again.

Pietro felt as if he had witnessed the Creation.

As he left the printing room, he reflected upon how far he had come. He had seen a great wonder. He had come up with an original idea. He was gainfully employed. He decided he would remain in Venice. The climate suited him and even if he could not be a poet, even if he could not have Sophia, at least he could be a little happy.

He was crossing the dockside whistling when he heard a sudden noise. A mighty blow struck the back of his head and he lost consciousness.

When he awoke he was on a boat in the middle of the Mediterranean Sea. Surrounded by pirates.

Thirteen

"Pirates?" I asked. "Seriously? Pirates?"

Giannotti appeared confused. "Do you have a problem with this?"

"If I wanted a plot development that would make this story even more preposterous than it already is, the only thing I could possibly come up with would be pirates."

"But that is what happened."

"You're sure about that."

"It's what was written in—"

"The notebook in the wine cask. Right. Though I suppose being captured by pirates is a fitting end for the man who invented vanity presses."

"Oh no. This is not the end of the story. Far from it. The notebook records—"

"Did it ever occur to you that someone might have made all this up?"

Giannotti's back stiffened. "Pietro Begnini is a Florentine hero. His story—"

"Has no point." I folded my arms across my chest, bracing against the evening chill. "And meanders. Can we jump to the climax?"

"I disagree that there is no point. Pietro found himself unable to write due to factors beyond his control. Does that not seem even a tiny bit familiar to you?"

I fell silent.

"Subsequently, Pietro was lost and directionless. Have you never had a similar experience?"

I didn't answer his question. "Proceed with your story." I shook my head. "Pirates. And then what, maybe the twelve labors of Hercules?"

Giannotti smiled. "That comes later."

PERHAPS A WORD OF EXPLANATION SHOULD BE PROVIDED ABOUT THE state of piracy in Pietro's day. The Barbary Coast had been a lucrative trade route for decades. Since Columbus' recent discovery of the New World, explorers from many European nations sent their ships across the Atlantic in search of treasure. And wherever there is treasure, there will be pirates. Some pirates will take the form of casino operators, preying on people's dreams. Some will take the form of fashion consultants, preying on people's insecurities. And some will take the form of divorce lawyers, but that is too ugly to be discussed in a story such as this. The pirates who captured Pietro took the form of large men on a sailing ship originating in North Africa and plundering the Mediterranean Sea.

When Pietro awoke, he was lying on the top deck of a galleon. Several heads peered down at him.

"Welcome aboard The Flying Frenchman," the tallest said. "I am Jean-David Neu, the legendary Flail of the Italians, the Scourge of the Seven Seas. Your captain and host." He sported a flowing black wig and a silken waistcoat. He held a silver-hilted cutlass that he gesticulated with as he spoke. "Perhaps you have heard of me? But of course you have. My exploits are legendary throughout the civilized world. I am renowned for my seamanship, *oui*, but especially for my bloodthirsty and unforgiving ways. Men still speak of the Battle of Trieste, during which I vanquished three other ships of larger size. My enemies were destroyed, their women taken for my pleasure and their children sold into slavery." He removed his feather hat with a flourish and bowed. "May I be of service?"

Pietro blinked several times. "Where—am I?"

"You are on a ship bound for the Straits of Magellan and from there to the great ocean beyond."

"But—*why* am I here?"

Neu twirled the end of his moustache between his fingers. "I am grieved to say you have been pressed into service."

"You are with the Gallic Navy?"

"No, we are a private firm. But we found ourselves short a few men during a brief respite in Venetia due to an outbreak of a disease which cannot be mentioned but is a common symptom of shore leave. Do not despair. Most men come to enjoy life on the high seas. There is freedom here. A chance for a man to be a man. The life of the corsair is exciting and rewarding. So long as you follow the rules and do your share of the work, you may find that you like it."

Pietro propped himself up on his arms. "But I had gainful employment in Venetia."

"I am sorry to inform you that your employment has been terminated."

"What will I do here? I know nothing of sailing."

Neu helped him to his feet and clapped him heartily on the back. "Fear not. It has been my experience that every man has talent, and those talents can always be of service aboard a sailing vessel. On one expedition, we captured a man who knew only masonry work. Never been to sea a day in his life. I put him to work building a captain's cabin. Worked wonderfully. Man wielded a blade like a platen, too. Fiery in combat. I pressed another man into service who'd been a great doge's manservant. I put him in charge of keeping the ship clean. He swabbed the deck and scraped the barnacles off the hull. Invaluable. Freed up other men for more bloodthirsty duties. You see, whatever your skills, whatever your talents, we'll find a way to put them to use on this mighty ship. So tell me, monsieur. What's your line?"

Pietro swallowed. "Poetry."

There was a protracted silence.

Neu batted his cutlass against the side of his head. "This could be more difficult than I imagined."

MEETINGS WERE HELD. BEHIND CLOSED DOORS. THE CAPTAIN AND the quartermaster, a rugged bald man named Rupert, considered possible options. It was too late to put to port and set Pietro free. The captain did not want to throw him into the ocean, but the first mate, an ambitious youth named Roberts, objected to having a man on board who did not contribute to the communal good. Quartermaster Rupert, usually the man most conservative about spending and thus most likely to want Pietro set adrift, was strangely silent. The others shouted and ranted and spoke in fearsome tones.

Pietro became increasingly concerned the longer the discussion continued. All his life he had heard about the dreaded Barbary pirates. Tales of pirate atrocities were often employed by mothers to induce obedience from their children. Now he found himself cast among them, helpless and undefended, utterly at their mercy.

True, he had left Leo seeking adventure. But now that he had found it, he feared he would not survive it.

At last the men emerged from the captain's quarters. "An accommodation has been reached," Captain Neu announced. "You are herewith employed as my personal valet."

Pietro was in no position to argue. "What will be my duties?"

Neu shrugged. "The usual valet duties."

"Such as?"

"The...dressing, grooming, food clearing...I don't know exactly. I've never had a valet. We will define your duties over time."

Pietro heard a grumbling from the other pirates.

Quartermaster Rupert was less dashing than Captain Neu, less physically fit, but somehow more frightening. "The new boy will be paid a minimum share. No eligibility for prize money for the first ninety days. No disability coverage."

That seemed to quiet the others somewhat.

"Disability coverage?" Pietro inquired.

"Indeed," Neu replied. "I don't know what you've heard about pirates, but we're an egalitarian bunch and we take care of our own. Our leadership principles are modeled after those of ancient Greece."

"The pirate ship is a democracy?"

"We are not afraid of dangerous notions. After all, we are pirates, no?" He made a hearty chuckling noise. "Each year, the captain and the quartermaster are chosen by a vote of the crewmen. Together, those two choose the other officers. The captain must be a fighting man like me, *oui*?" He removed his cutlass with a flourish and swished it through the air. "The quartermaster must be good with numbers. He must divide the booty in a fair manner. Each man receives a share according to his contribution and seniority. A portion of all captured goods are set aside, however, to create a common fund used to compensate crew members who are injured in combat. Or their families. One hundred pieces of eight for the loss of an eye. Six hundred pieces of eight for the loss of a leg. And so forth."

"Quite fair," Pietro commented.

"No organization can consider itself civilized without some form of universal coverage for health issues and loss. We're pirates, not barbarians."

"I see that."

Neu clapped his hands together. "So we'll finish the paper-work, and then you can begin your pirate duties. I like a cup of Earl Grey at four in the afternoon. Piping hot. Dinner at eight. I take my bath at ten."

"I'll see to it."

PIETRO EMBRACED HIS NEW PIRATE DUTIES WITH ALMOST THE SAME energy he had applied to his work at the Academy. He saw no opportunity to escape, so he thought he should make the best of the situation. As it turned out, Captain Neu was not a difficult master. He was unaccustomed to having someone pamper him and didn't particularly like it. This caused Pietro to like him all the more, as he had clearly invented this valet job to prevent Pietro from being thrown overboard.

There was one cabin on the lowest level of the ship that Pietro was not allowed to enter, not even allowed to approach. From time to time, he heard strange muffled sounds emanating from within. The sound was at once both pitiable and fearsome.

The cabin was guarded by two men at all times. Pietro could see the door was triple-locked and barred. What was in there? he wondered. But his captain had warned him to stay away, so he complied.

After his third week of valeting, as he cleared the captain's dinner, he worked up the nerve to ask Neu about the mysterious locked cabin.

"You are not to go anywhere near there!" Neu bellowed.

"I know. I didn't. But I can hear the sounds. There is some-thing unnatural about it."

"Keep your mind on your duties, valet."

"I perform my duties. But what is it you have locked up?" Pietro knew it would be wiser not to press. But he had a poet's curiosity about all things, and he had ventured forth to gain knowledge of the world, after all. "Is it some exotic beast?"

"No."

"Some hideous monster?'

"No."

"Then what?"

Captain Neu turned away and then, all at once, dropped to his knees as if in prayer, hands clasped together. "It is a beautiful woman. The love of my life. The woman for whom I would give all, do anything." His head fell. "I asked for her hand in marriage. But she would not have me."

"So you locked her up?"

"It's complicated."

"Was this intended to change her mind?"

"No. She has told me repeatedly that nothing would ever change her mind. We are from two different worlds, she says. She is a member of a high-born family tree, only three twigs from Louis himself. And I am a pirate."

"Perhaps if you renounced piracy."

"And did what?"

"Captained a ship for a legitimate trading company?"

"You want me to work for the man. *Mon dieu*! No one ever got rich working for someone else."

"Then I suppose you are faced with a choice. Fortune or happiness."

"But I want both!"

"You cannot have both."

"There must be some way I can woo her. Bring her to her senses. Some way she might see me as something other than a rascal. I would give anything to the man who could deliver her hand to me." He rose. "But alas, it is impossible."

Pietro raised a finger. "Are we dead?"

"I think we are not."

"Then it is not impossible. I have been told by the wisest man alive that nothing is impossible for the imaginative mind."

"Very well then. You tell me how I can win my lady's love. Give me the answer and perhaps I will one day give you your freedom."

Pietro opted not to tell Neu about his own miserable failure in the playing fields of love. "You are asking a woman to go against her instincts. To rebel against everything she has ever valued."

"As I say, impossible."

"No. Difficult, but not impossible. To succeed, you must employ the one thing, the one and only wondrous magical thing that no woman, regardless of her background or nationality or station, can resist."

"Jewels?"

"No, no."

"Flattery?"

"No."

"Amorous expertise?"

"Not at all."

"Then what?"

Pietro smiled. "Poetry."

Fourteen

A nd that is how Pietro was transformed from the most useless man on the pirate ship to the most indispensable man Captain Neu had ever met. He offered the captain the one weapon he had never before possessed. Neu was hostile at first, saying that a manly pirate had no need for sissy stuff like poetry. He was a man of action, not of words. But the woman locked on the lower deck—Madame the Baroness Eloise du Pontmercy—continued to dismiss his requests, threats, and deprivations. So in desperation, he turned to Pietro. And poetry.

Since the captain was not a poetical soul, and in point of fact did not even read or write, he was entirely dependent upon Pietro. At that point, for all practical purposes, the captain became Pietro's valet.

"The most important thing," Pietro said, "is that she believes the poetry is coming from you. And that you are writing from your heart."

"Fine, fine. You write it down and I'll give it to her."

"No. She would see through that ruse immediately. She would know it was not in your hand. And even if she did not, she would expect you to be able to speak as poetically as you write. My captain, you must become an educated man."

As it turned out, there was no great hurry about this matter. Despite being locked in the hold, Madame du Pontmercy was well-treated and well-provided for. Her isolation was not a punishment but a lifestyle choice. She had no desire to mix with pirates and there was no other company to be had at the moment. Pietro calculated that it would take about three months to reach the New World, six months or so to plunder it, and three more months to return. Not coincidentally, he calculated that Captain Neu's education would take exactly that long. In effect, he created a permanent position for himself, one that ensured that he would not be set adrift and that he would be safe at all times.

"When we return," he told the captain, "you will have captured your lady's heart."

First, the captain had to learn his letters. As it turned out, there was not that much for the captain to do on a pirate ship when they were not attacking anyone, so the lessons proceeded briskly. Neu proved a clever and highly motivated student.

Next, he instructed his captain on the fundamentals of reading and writing, using poetry as text whenever possible. He wanted the captain to be as infused with poetry as he himself had been when he studied at the Academy. He hoped that eventually Neu would compose poetry of his own. Neu did not, after all, have to come up with an original metaphor. He just had to win the hand of a woman who had been locked in a cabin for months.

Pietro copied out long passages of classical poetry from memory. Neu absorbed them with fervor. He asked questions about everything from scansion to symbolism. He remained in his cabin for hours at a time, studying.

One day not long after their passage through the Strait, Quartermaster Rupert asked Pietro to take the captain a message.

He found the captain hunched over his writing desk.

"Sir, the quartermaster tells me—"

"I am troubled by this passage from Dante."

"Sir, an enemy ship—"

"He seems to use the same trite tropes *ad nauseum*. I want to problematize this elementary conceptualization of sin and punishment."

"Sir, it is a royal cruiser from the Spanish Armada. It is moving at a rapid pace—"

"Pietro, are you listening to me? I'm talking about Dante. Who I must say I am finding rather trying."

"Sir, the quartermaster believes this could be the greatest prize ship in the world."

"Such repetition. Sin. Punishment. Sin. Punishment. And all so obvious. The flatterers are thrown into a pit of human excrement. The soothsayers have their heads twisted so they can only see the past. The Tower of Babel's builder is forced to speak a language no one understand."

"Sir, that is known as poetic justice."

"It just seems like bad writing to me. Masking the hard questions under a veneer of cheap irony. And listen to this passage: 'They had their faces twisted toward their haunches/and found it necessary to walk backward.' The scansion is off. He got the dactyls wrong. Sneaking in an extra beat where it has no place. He's cheating to make the terza rima work."

"Sir, I believe your attention is required on deck."

"I had hoped to incorporate this three-lined stanza into my own masterwork. But my poem remains unfinished. And now I question the entire endeavor."

"As do I, sir. You must—"

"Perhaps a dimeter spondee would do as well. Or a choriamb. Challenging, of course, what with the four-syllable metric foot with a stressed syllable followed by two unstressed syllables and closing with a stressed syllable. But I think I'm up to it. And the Madame would surely be impressed by the technical prowess involved." He sighed. "I'm having a great deal of trouble with my final stanza."

"Sir," Pietro said, raising his voice as loudly as a valet could dare. "The Spanish ship will soon be in carronade range. The quartermaster believes we should attack. But even if we do not, the Spanish ship will surely attack us. Your presence is required on the deck."

"Oh bother," Neu said, crumpling his parchment between his fingers. "The creative mind should be free of these tedious quotidian duties." He pushed away from his desk. "Very well. Back to the salt mines."

Pietro led him to the deck. A storm raged, sending sheets of rain upon them. The entire crew awaited instructions, loaded down with muskets and cutlasses. In the distance, through a thick mist of sea spray, Pietro perceived the Spanish ship approaching.

Neu approached Quartermaster Rupert. "Status report?"

He spoke in low tones. "The wind is with the enemy, sir. But we are maintaining our position. I've stationed men on the oars to hold us in place. The storm began at two bells. It's worse now. The teeming waves are a hindrance, but I believe we have the better position. I've seen the enemy ship yaw and sag, falling sideways to such an extreme that the launch and the cutter dragged, stern first after her wavering bows. Based upon careful measurement with the sextant, I am able to say that in the next five minutes she will be within range. We've loaded the eighteen-pounders, but the carronades will not be useful until we are much closer. As soon as the enemy's mizzenmast comes into view, we should—" He paused. "Captain, are you listening?"

Neu started. "What? Oh, sorry. I was trying to think of a word that rhymes with 'plank.'"

Rupert grasped him by the shoulders. "Captain! Do you order an attack?"

"I don't quite know. Apparently men of violence are destined for the fourth circle of hell. According to *Il Supremo Poeta*—"

"Captain! We need orders."

Pietro sidled up to the captain and whispered. "Sir, if this ship is seized, the Spanish will capture Madame du Pontmercy.

You will likely never see her again. Which means of course—" Here he paused for dramatic effect. "—she will never read your poem."

Captain Neu's teeth, all eight of them, clenched tightly together. "Mister Quartermaster. Launch the attack."

THE LONG AND HORRIBLE BATTLE TOOK MOST OF THE DAY, BUT WHEN at last the smoke cleared and the blood washed off the deck, Captain Neu and his crew stood victorious. Pietro was impressed by the fighting on both sides. The Spaniards were dogged and valorous, but perhaps not as experienced. Still, they fought to the last man and accounted themselves well. By the time the battle ended, splintered timbers were all that remained of the aged Spanish ship. Neu sent his crew aboard to loot. After they finished, he ordered a hasty withdrawal. He feared the flames on the Spanish ship would eventually reach the powder charges in the magazine, and when they did, the ship would explode.

Afterward, Pietro was summoned to the quartermaster's quarters.

Pietro knew the quartermaster was popularly known as Rupert Rumbelly, though he suspected that nickname was not much used while the booty was being distributed. Rupert had a desk, but it was piled high with ledgers and ink. An abacus rested at the far corner.

"I have a bone to pick with you, poet," Rupert growled. "The captain seems not himself."

"No," Pietro agreed. "He does not."

"Some say you are to blame."

"I hope not."

"Some people claim there's a woman to blame."

Pietro tilted his head to one side. "Ye-es. I believe the captain is enamored of the captive. The Madame du Pontmercy."

Rupert Rumbelly shook his massive head. "I might have known. Always bad to have a woman on board. Ne'er portends well." He gave Pietro a long and probing look. "Are you aware that we have a by-election coming on the first of the month?"

"A by-election?"

"The captaincy is up for grabs."

Pietro felt a trembling though his spine. This could ruin all his plans. "Were you, uh, thinking of running for the captaincy?"

"Why would I take a demotion? The quartermaster controls the purse. The captain is just a figurehead. A hooligan to lead the men into battle. More likely to die than get rich." He paused. "Still, an unwise captain can create a serious financial deficit."

"I ...don't quite follow."

"We've been spending more than we make for some time now. Running up debt. Borrowing from the moneylenders of Trieste. Bad policy. You can't keep raising the debt ceiling. Got to reduce your expenditures. Get a balanced budget. Otherwise the whole operation crashes under its own weight. We're robbing our children, that's what we're doing. Did you see that battle today?"

"Indeed, sir. A glorious encounter."

"It was anything but. If we'd captured the ship, we could have collected prize money from the Spanish government. But there is no money for a ship burned to bits. That's the problem with Neu and his oh-so-fearsome reputation. People think he will take no prisoners, so they fight to the finish, which usually results in nothing being left when the battle is over. If people thought he would take prisoners, they might surrender and we could avoid all the fuss. We've had no prize money for over a year. Barely any booty worth mentioning."

"You did capture the Baroness."

"Yes, a worthless woman whose family has refused to pay ransom. We should have thrown her to the sharks a long time ago. Another bad decision by a captain who needs to be retired.

I'm putting one of my close associates, the first mate Roberts, up for the captaincy."

"Why are you telling me this?"

"Isn't it obvious? I want your support in the election." He gave Pietro a wink. "I can make things nice for you around here, son. Better hammock. Larger rum ration. Maybe an extra share of the booty now and again. You be my friend and I'll be yours."

"Are you trying to buy my vote?"

"Of course not. But the men respect you. And your opinion."

"They do?"

"You're an Academy man. They know that. If you tell them it's time for a change, they'll listen."

"I don't know…"

"Give it some thought, son." He clapped Pietro on the shoulder. "We could use a man like you in our administration." His voice dropped a few notches. "But we will have no use for a valet who can't be trusted."

"I'm not really a valet, sir. I want to be a poet."

Rupert shivered. "I hate poetry. Can't understand a word of it. Think all poets should be keelhauled. Why can't people just say what they mean, without all the code words and symbols? If you have something to say, say it already, that's my thinking."

"I grasp your point, but—"

"What is it with all this weak-kneed prancing about with pretty words? Why do women like that? Is a poem going to put food on their table? Is a poem going to protect them from the barbarian hordes? Is a poet going to know how to make them feel like a woman?"

"Well, opinions differ…"

Rupert inhaled deeply. "Now writing stories—that's a man's game. None of this pantywaist rhyming nonsense. Just a rip-snorting good adventure filled with blood and entrails and close shaves and suspense and running and jumping and fighting and making love and perhaps a word or two about the Holy Grail at the end. Something to thrill the mind and chill the bones. That's a man's book."

"I see. Perhaps I should return to my duties—"

Rupert opened his lowest desk drawer. "As a matter of fact, I have a manuscript I've been tinkering with on the odd moment. Would you be willing to read it?"

Fifteen

P ietro left the quartermaster filled with concern. His safety on this ship rested with the captain, in whom he had invested much time and education. If Neu were voted out of office, it would not matter whether he won his lady. A lame-duck pirate captain can provide little security.

Even if the captain remained captain, Pietro was lost if Neu's amorous pursuits failed. Perhaps the captain would survive, just as Pietro had struggled on after he lost Sophia. But Pietro had a strength in his heart that came from his unquenchable desire to be a poet. Captain Neu had a strength of his own, to be sure, but whether it would bear him through an amorous disaster, Pietro did not know. And what the consequences of that failure might be, he could not predict. He could only worry.

He entered the captain's cabin and found him scribbling furiously at his desk. Neu had not changed or even washed since the battle. His face was black with soot and his uniform was stained with blood.

"Pietro! Where have you been? I think I've got this poem finished. I use the image of the sinking Spanish ship as a metaphor for the fire burning in my heart: *La Navidad* is gone / A volcano burning on the sea / But my love burns and shall / For it longs to burn with thee." He jumped up, eyes wide. "What do you think? Do you like it? I like it. At least I think I like it. Do you think she will like it?"

Neu slapped the poem down on his desktop. "I'm concerned about the switch from terza rima to iambic pentameter. Do you think it loses some of its complexity? I want her to perceive my work as serious literature, not accessible hackwork. I'm also concerned about the voice. I didn't want to sound too casual, if you know what I mean. Too lacy shirt without the ruffles. This is the work of an educated man, after all. I have no idea what my lady's educational background might be."

Pietro cleared his throat. "I think she will be flattered that you made the attempt."

"And what about this second stanza? Where I extend the volcano trope and talk about the 'obbligato of fire.' Do you think that works? Can there be an obbligato of fire? Am I trying too hard?"

"So long as she feels emotions stirring—"

"And is there too much death? Is it too scary? Or too suggestive? I mean, we all know what a volcano symbolizes."

"I often dream of volcanoes."

"I'm not surprised. But focus on my poem, Pietro. What about the business with the mizzenmast? I love the way that word sounds, don't you? *Mizzenmast.* I could say that all night long. Rolls off the tongue. But I'm not sure the nautical imagery lands. I may have two poems here. Or even three."

"I think it's fine as it is."

"Perhaps I should say the clouds drift by looking like a mizzenmast. Can clouds look like mizzenmasts? Have I overdone the mizzenmasts?" He snapped his fingers. "Maybe that's the title. 'Mizzenmast.' That would be a nice bit of symbolism, hinting at the resolution in the final stanza when the narrator— ostensibly *moi*—likens himself to a deity fueled by the affection of the beloved reader. Am I right? Or is that just the way I read it? What do you think?"

"I think I have created a monster," Pietro said quietly. "My captain—just give her the poem. She'll either like it or she won't. Let's find out."

Neu pivoted, pressing his hand against his forehead. "I cannot. I am too embarrassed. It is presumptuous to assume she would even wish to read it."

"Was that not the whole point of writing it?"

"I am unworthy."

Pietro snatched the poem from the desk. "Then I shall take it to her."

I SHOULD MENTION THAT MADAME THE BARONESS ELOISE DU Pontmercy was born to a titled and landed French family. Like most women of that time, she had not received a classical education, but she was learned in the womanly arts, primarily sewing and cookery and playing the virginal. Her father's investments went sour and he was forced to pursue risky enterprises in the New World. Since she was not yet betrothed, it was decided, much to her dismay, that she would follow her father to the French settlements on the new continent. While in transit, her father's ship was attacked by Captain Neu and his band of pirates. The ship burned, but they managed to save the Madame at the last possible moment.

In truth, she had few complaints. She was treated better on this ship than she had been on the one before, and she had been promised passage to France on their return voyage, which she much preferred to the New World, especially now that her father had been eliminated. His estates in France were still in the family name but deeply in debt. Without the income he hoped to secure in the New World, they seemed destined to fall into the hands of creditors. But she was confident that, being of the aristocracy and being quite beautiful—something would turn up.

She was not expecting that it would be a young man in tattered clothing who worked as the captain's valet.

PIETRO STEPPED PAST THE GUARDS AND ENTERED MADAME DU Pontmercy's cell. The heavy door closed behind him. They were alone together.

For someone who'd been without visitors for months, she was not particularly interested in his arrival.

She wore the white flowing wig and billowing dress popular in France at that time. Her face was powdered and she wore a single black beauty mark on her left cheek. Her cell was lavishly appointed with soft pillows and upholstered chairs. She spoke slowly and tended to emphasize each syllable of every word. "I do not recall indicating that I was receiving visitors."

"I am the captain's valet," Pietro said, standing awkwardly before her on the opposite end of the cell.

"About time. My laundry is in the corner. No starch."

"You misunderstand. I'm here to read a poem."

"Oh." She flipped open a fan. "If you must. Proceed."

Pietro began. "*La Navidad* is gone / A volcano burning on the sea / But my love burns and shall / For it longs to burn with thee...."

Pietro read every stanza. All in all, he thought it fairly accomplished, especially for a scribe who had only recently been introduced to poetry or, for that matter, the alphabet. He did think the cloud imagery was a bit tiresome and the euphony suffered from an excessive use of the word "mizzenmast." Still, not a bad effort. He hoped the Baroness would be impressed.

"That is the conclusion of the reading, Madame," he said, bowing slightly. "I would like to add—"

He got no further. Madame du Pontmercy launched herself at him, knocking him to the ground and smothering him in wet hot kisses.

"Madame! You misapprehend!"

She did not stop. She kissed his lips, his eyes, his nose. She pulled his hair with unbridled passion.

He pushed himself away. "Madame. I have misled you. I only read the poem. It was composed by the captain. He nurtures a great and abiding affection for you."

She laughed, blew a strand of hair out of her face, then launched herself at him again.

"Madame, please! The captain—"

"Hush already about the captain," she said, pinning Pietro down. "Do you take me for a fool? I heard that the captain captured a poet and that is obviously you."

"Yes, but—"

"I attempted to make conversation with your captain when he brought me on board. It was evident he had no schooling. He could not even write his own name."

"Yes, but—"

"So quiet yourself. You have won my heart, my soul, and my body with your words. Take what is yours. Show me no mercy. I am French, after all."

It took Pietro almost ten minutes to pry himself away from her. He pounded on the door, pleading for release. At last the guards let him out.

He saw himself in a looking glass. His hair was a mess. Lipstick and powder smeared his face. His clothes were untucked and torn. His breeches dangled around his knees.

He heard the sound of a throat clearing.

Captain Neu stood behind him, staring, mouth agape.

"Captain!"

Neu drew his cutlass. "Prepare to die."

Sixteen

C aptain Neu rushed Pietro, shoving him against the bulkhead, pressing his cutlass to Pietro's throat. "It seems my poem was a success."

His eyes lowered. "Well...the meter is a bit off in the fifth stanza."

"You dare defile my lady?"

"There was very little defiling. I mean, none really."

"And you use my own words to accomplish your foul deed!"

"I didn't mean—I didn't want to go in there in the first place. I only went because you would not."

"And that is your excuse for deflowering the sweetest baroness who ever walked the face of the earth?"

"I did nothing! She attacked me!"

"You expect me to believe you were attacked by that gentle woman? Those lips that never before felt a man's touch?"

"I am not altogether sure about that."

"And you used my poem to accomplish your insidious goal!"

The blade pressed against Pietro's windpipe, making it difficult to breathe, much less speak. "I told her you wrote the poem. She did not believe me."

"Because, I suppose, I am such an uneducated meathead that no one would ever believe I wrote a poem."

"Well…"

Neu pulled away from Pietro as suddenly as he had attacked, his head drooping. "And now I am lost. Even if I throw you to the sharks, as well I should, it would not bring my lady back to me. My one chance to win her has passed."

"Perhaps if you wrote another poem."

"She would think it came from you."

"Perhaps if you read it yourself."

"She would still think it came from you."

"Perhaps if you composed it while she watched."

"She would think you wrote it and I memorized it. No, it is impossible. I will never win her affection."

Pietro rubbed his sore throat. "Did you ever consider just… wooing her?"

"Wooing? What is wooing?"

"You know. Calling on her. Asking her out. Following the rules of courtship and etiquette."

"I am a pirate, not some simpering whimpering wooer!"

"I have read that women like being wooed."

"I have lived many lives on many shores of many nations. And in none of them did I ever woo."

"But you were willing to try poetry. Why not wooing? If you wooed, you might learn new and private details about her. Then you could incorporate this knowledge into a poem while she watched. And then she would know it could only have been composed by you."

"This is foolishness. I do not think I have another poem in me. I am not some hack who churns out words every day. I only write from inspiration. The inspiration is gone." He inflated his chest. "And a pirate captain does not woo."

Pietro shrugged. "Then I guess you're right. The Baroness is lost."

Neu fell silent. His eyes smoldered. His fists balled up. He shook with rage.

And then, at last, he placed his cutlass back in its scabbard. "How is it done, this wooing?"

Pietro knew precious little about it himself. He and Sophia had loved one another almost immediately, and that had not turned out well, so he could hardly call himself an expert. But he had spent his entire life reading poetry, roughly four-fifths of which concerned love. So he shared what he knew.

He taught Neu how to bow politely, how to kiss a lady's hand without actually making contact. They practiced flattery, double entendres, and devilish innuendos. He showed Neu how to let a lady take his arm and, perhaps most difficult of all, how to dance—a skill Pietro acquired while traveling with Leo. He told Neu how to make eye contact when his lady spoke, how to make her feel as if nothing existed in his entire world but her.

At last, he felt Neu was ready for his first date. Neu dressed in his most elaborate outfit, a frilled satin coat, a plumed hat, and a sash bearing the names of all his sea conquests. The ship had no chocolate, so instead he brought an extra helping of hardtack, seasoned with rare spices from Cathay. He had no flowers, but he made an admirable effort at arranging kelp.

Pietro walked with Neu to the Madame's bolted door, reviewing all the niceties as they walked. Bow. Kiss. Flatter. Hint. Dance. Poetry.

"Do you feel confident?" Pietro asked.

"No, I feel terrified. But a pirate captain does not shirk from a challenge. Even one that appears impossible."

"But nothing—"

Neu raised a hand. "I know. Nothing is impossible to the imaginative mind."

He knocked on her door.

The Baroness allowed him to enter.

Pietro remained outside, as he wanted no indication that he had played any role in the proceedings therein.

Captain Neu remained in her cabin for over three hours.

And when at last he left, well past midnight, he smiled. His cheeks were ruddy and flushed.

Pietro pulled him aside. "How did it go?"

"I do not wish to…how you say…kiss and tell. But I think the lady does not altogether hate me."

"That is wonderful."

"Of course, I never had any doubt," Neu said, twirling the end of his moustache. "I am, after all, her lord and master. I am the Scourge of the Seven Seas, the most fearsome captain of the greatest pirate ship—"

"About that," Pietro said. "We need to talk. There's a by-election in a few days."

Neu tossed his ruffled hand into the air. "A trifle. After my stunning conquests, no one would dare run against me."

"I have it on good authority that your first mate will run against you. He has the support of the quartermaster. And the men are always readily influenced by the man who pays them."

Neu's brow creased. "That is true."

"I also know booty has been scarce of late. And when the economy is poor, voters vote for change."

"The audacity of Rupert. I remember when he was a hopeless rummy wallowing in the gutter of a French bordello. I was the one who gave him a chance. I was the one who bought him his first abacus. The ingratitude!" Neu's eyes narrowed. "And whose side be you on, poet?"

"Yours, of course." About this, Pietro was being completely honest. With Captain Neu, he felt he had a chance of returning home one day. He had not forgotten that Rupert wanted to throw him overboard the first day he arrived. Besides, Rupert's manuscript was unsalvageable, and he did not relish being the one to tell him so.

"Do you think I can beat the first mate? Despite the economy?"

"I think it is possible. You might have one thing he does not have."

"My battle experience?"

"No."

"My *savior faire?*"

"No."

"My fearful countenance?"

"Yes, but that will not help you."

"What then? What is it I might have that he does not? Poetry?"

Pietro shook his head. "A first lady."

A DEBATE BETWEEN THE CANDIDATES WAS SCHEDULED FOR ELECTION day. Negotiations with the Baroness began immediately. Captain Neu returned to her chambers, this time bringing Pietro to serve as witness and amanuensis.

"I will not be the consort of a pirate!" the Baroness exclaimed.

Neu took her hand, alternating kisses and supplications. "My lady, I do not ask for your hand as yet. Only your promise."

"It is ridiculous. I come from one of the finest families in France."

"And I am the finest pirate on the water. I have conquered everyone there is to conquer!"

"It is hardly the same thing."

"Would you not rather be with a manly pirate than some prancing dandy?"

She lowered her veil. "Those are not my only two choices."

"You were affectionate enough when last we met."

"What did you expect? I've been locked up here for months. And your poet wasn't interested."

"We could be a power couple. King and queen of the Spanish Main."

"Not if you lose the election."

"Then help me win the election."

"No!"

They both folded their arms across their chests.

"We are at an impasse," Neu pronounced.

"So it would seem."

Pietro cleared his throat. "May I make a suggestion?" He had watched them carefully throughout the encounter. Despite the fact that the two barely knew one another, their dispute reminded him of nothing so much as the battles he had witnessed between his parents. They sometimes argued for hours. But when they were finished, they gave Pietro money to go to a puppet show and locked themselves behind their bedroom door.

"I have heard you mention, Madame, that you are from one of the finest families in all of France."

"True," she snapped.

"And I have heard you mention, Captain, that you have conquered everyone there is to conquer."

"Also true," he replied.

"Then it would seem to me that you are both at a career crossroads. You, Madame, are from a fine family, but the family is penniless. You, Captain, are a fine pirate, but there is nothing piratical you have not already done."

The Madame looked at the pirate. The pirate looked at the Madame.

Pietro continued. "You may be from a fine family, Madame, but that family has no lineal male heir, correct?"

"Sadly, yes."

"And in France, wealth cannot pass to a woman. Since you have no offspring or husband, the family fortune will pass to an uncle or perhaps a cousin."

She covered her mouth. "Cousin Percy, the inebriate!"

"I assume no action has yet been taken, as you have not delivered the news of your father's demise. But you cannot delay that forever. It would be well if when you make that announcement…you have a husband. Someone who could inherit the land and the estates."

Her chin slowly rose. "But since my father has already died, this marriage would come after the fortune has legally passed to my cousin."

"Not necessarily. A common-law marriage might have begun the moment the two of you cohabited the same ship. Who is to say?"

Neu's eyes narrowed. "If you do not succeed in your quest to become a poet, Pietro, I suggest you consider a career in law."

"But what of the debts on the estate?" Madame said. "If they are not paid we will lose the property."

"And if I'm not mistaken," Pietro said, "the captain has a considerable retirement fund buried in a chest somewhere in the Hebrides, correct?"

Neu tilted his head. "*Oui.*"

"So you pay the debts. You marry the Madame and receive her family estate and all the income derived therefrom. You give up the pirate life which has begun to bore you anyway and become a gentleman of distinction with a beautiful, aristocratic wife."

"But I will lose my rights to that retirement fund if I lose the captaincy."

"Then you must not lose. I would suggest an immediate nuptial. As the captain of a seafaring vessel, I believe you can delegate the authority to perform marriages to an associate. Like me. And then the two of you join the campaign trail together." He smiled. "Because behind every great man there is a great woman."

THE REPRESENTATIVES OF THE TWO CANDIDATES DETERMINED THE terms of the debate. Captain Neu favored a formal format in which they would take turns orating. Roberts favored a looser structure with questions taken from the crew and more interaction between the candidates. Being a member of the crew, he undoubtedly thought he would be better at relating to them. They settled on a format that incorporated both approaches.

The debate took place on the stern deck, topside. Every available man attended. The two candidates stood on either side of the mainmast. Rupert sat nearest to Roberts, thereby demonstrating his support. Beside Neu was his new bride, beaming at him. She understandably attracted a great deal of notice. Whether this would help Neu, or simply draw attention from him, Pietro was uncertain.

The debate began in a predictable manner. "Listen to the voice of experience," Captain Neu implored his men. "These are treacherous times. There has never been more activity at sea, nor more men of bad character anxious to rob an honest pirate of his hard-earned wages. We should not change horses midstream. You need the wisdom and experience that can only come from a man who has dedicated his life to the service of his fellow pirates."

Roberts had a different approach. "We need change! We demand change!" He repeated the word over and over again as if it answered all questions. "Swab the deck clean. Inject new blood. Wisdom isn't about age and experience. It's about what a pirate has where it matters. Our revenues are down and you all know it. We've burned too many ships and pillaged too few. The quartermaster has been forced to resort to deficit spending to provision the ship. We must balance the budget. Otherwise we shortchange ourselves and future generations."

"What is all this talk of money?" Neu cut in, as permitted by the flexible format. "Are we pirates or moneylenders? Our job is to rob and pillage, not to blather on about the budget."

"Easy for you to say," Roberts countered. "You've got your retirement fund tucked away somewhere. But what of the rest of us? We haven't had prize money for more than a year. Our wages have been suspended. We haven't had a rum ration in over a month. We're down to hardtack and gruel. Perhaps your fund should be converted to the greater good."

"I've contributed my share to the commonweal."

"You should contribute more. You have more."

"Everyone should be taxed equally."

"Those who are better able to pay should contribute a larger percentage."

Neu pounded the mast. "This is a pirate ship, not a rest home for the poor and infirm."

"We'll all be poor and infirm if we let you lead us."

The debate continued in this unproductive manner for some time. Pietro did not know what to do. He understood poems, not politics. But he could tell Neu was losing. At one point, the Baroness actually swayed a bit, tugging her dress lower, exposing a bit of shoulder. The men were appreciative, but it did not appear to increase the captain's approval rating.

"Discipline has fallen off," Roberts insisted. "Sloppy discipline leads to sloppy pirating. And sloppy profits. We barely survived that last attack. Where was the captain when we needed him? He had his head in the clouds. And he wasn't the only one. I know a crewman who cowered on the lower deck of the ship during the entire fight. I know another who hid from danger by pretending to have a broken arm. I know a crewman who hasn't taken his turn at fishing for over a month. What is the use of a captain who cannot maintain discipline, who spends all his time in his cabin scribbling?"

"I have done no such thing," Neu protested.

"Do you deny the charge that others have shirked their duties?"

Neu fluffed back his wig. "I am aware there have been some…lapses. Mistakes were made."

Roberts pointed a finger at him. "What do you intend to do about it?"

Neu coughed into his ruffled sleeve. "Well, we, er—"

"They should hang from the yardarm, that's what should happen!" The crowd cheered Roberts's murderous suggestion.

Behind him, Pietro saw the quartermaster fold his arms contentedly. He thought he had the election sewn up.

"*Sacre bleu*," Neu said. "That sounds a trifle extreme."

"That's what I would do," Roberts bellowed, "if I were captain. You have a clear choice, mates. You can have a captain who takes charge of the situation. Or you can continue to have a captain who does nothing!"

More deafening cheers from the onlookers. Pietro felt desperate. There must be some solution. But what was it? How could he help?

And then it came to him.

He edged beside Neu, pretending to bring him an important message. Then he turned his head so no others could see and whispered, "Poetry."

The captain gave him a penetrating, are-you-out-of-your-head look. "This is not the time for love ballads and odes to daffodils," he hissed.

"Poetic *justice*," Pietro hissed back. He left the deck.

Captain Neu contemplated.

Roberts continued talking. "It takes a strong man with a strong hand to make a pirate ship profitable. Shirkers must be punished to the fullest extent possible, and this captain is unwilling to do what must be done. He—"

Neu interrupted. "You misinform the crew. I said I would not hang the misbehaving men. A captain must have some sense about these things. We're pirates, not barbarians. Do we want the world to see us as butchers?"

A quiet murmur from the crowd.

"Do we want to be remembered as the crew that gave pirating a bad name?"

A louder murmur. Scattered rumblings.

"Not on my watch," Neu said firmly.

"Then what would you do?" a crewman cried out.

"I would—and will—issue punishments appropriate to the crime. I would mete out justice, not retribution. For the man who hid cravenly in the lowest berth of the ship—I would tie him to the highest crow's nest. And leave him there for days!"

A few of the men chuckled.

"For the man who feigned injury to hide from the battle, I would put him in the boxing ring and make him battle all comers, non-stop, no holds barred."

A louder cry from the men. Some whistled enthusiastically.

"And for the man who would not bait a hook—let him become the bait!"

The crew cheered wildly. They waved their tricorns in the air.

"Dangle him from the plank with a net. If he catches a fish, fine. And if a fish catches him—so be it!"

The response was staggering. Waves of appreciation cascaded toward him. Neu removed his hat and bowed. Like any good politician, he knew when it was time to exit.

Pietro covered his smile with his hand. It seemed Captain Neu had learned something from Dante after all.

THE VOTE WAS OVERWHELMINGLY IN CAPTAIN NEU'S FAVOR. PIETRO brokered a deal with the disgruntled Roberts and the quartermaster. They allowed Neu to take one half of the retirement fund now in exchange for an early retirement effective when they reached the French shore. Neu retained more than enough to pay the debts on the Baroness's estates. And Roberts would become captain after all, as soon as they left France.

When the day for their departure arrived, the Baroness clasped Pietro's hand in gratitude.

"I want to thank you for all you have done for us."

"It has been a pleasure to serve, Madame."

"The Captain"—she continued to call him that, even decades

into their marriage—"told me something of your plight. I don't know if you still seek to become a poet—"

"I do."

"Then take this." She gave him a piece of paper. "I do not know this man's current location. He is rumored to live alone somewhere in the hills of Tuscany. But I believe him to be the finest poet—and the finest teacher of poetry—alive today. If he cannot help you—"

"Then perhaps I will return to a life of piracy," Pietro said with a wink.

"I hope not," she replied. "I think you are destined for great things. But men only accomplish great things when they follow their heart."

Seventeen

D r. Giannotti stretched his legs. "The portion of my story involving Leo and Aldus and Lucy and the pirates was revealed in those vat-soaked journals composed in mirror-writing inscribed from right to left by the mad genius of Vinci, a leftie who took out his anger and resentment toward the right-handed majority by journaling in a hand only a mother could love. The next portion of the tale was even harder to uncover. Well into the twentieth century, no one knew where Pietro was for the remaining five of his so-called missing years. My grandfather was stymied by this dearth of information for many years, until one day by chance, deep in the bowels of one of Florence's oldest libraries, he found a torn scrap of paper with an enigmatic inscription:

ASK VITO TO TEACH YOU.

"Of course, in Florence, for a historian, there is only one Vito, that being Vito the Vituperative."

"Of course," I replied.

"Although the Grand Inquisitor was the master of all Florentine poetry in Pietro's day, he was only ranked 2nd in the contemporary poetical hierarchy. That is because the first-ranked of his kind left the Academy to live as a hermit in the Tuscan hills, alone and apart from what he called 'the scourge of prosaic mankind.' For a poet to call someone 'prosaic' was the greatest of all possible insults, even worse than being called a son of a tax collector. It is only logical that, if the Madame du Pontmercy sent Pietro in search of a tutor, it would be Vito the Vituperative.

"My grandfather wrote to Vito's only surviving descendant, a niece several times removed, who allowed him to review the family archives in exchange for bail money. My grandfather spent weeks at this task, poring through the dusty mildewed files in the bowels of the family tomb, until at long last he found a small enchiridion on manners and clean living. Someone had scrawled on the title page:

ASSIGNMENT BOOK
PIETRO BEGNINI, WOULD-BE POET.

"You can imagine how my grandfather's heart soared. Because on the facing page of this guidebook he found what amounted to a near-complete record of what happened during Pietro's tutelage under Vito the Vituperative. Finally, the last of the missing years were documented.

"As it turns out, Pietro spent more than a year searching, following tiny clues and rumors, before he discovered Vito the Vituperative residing in decidedly modest quarters. He lived in a cave on the side of a mighty Tuscan hill, the same cave in which later researchers would find earthenware jars containing the Lost Scrolls of Ambrose. But—"

"Let me guess," I interjected. "That is a story for another day."

Giannotti settled back into his chair. "Just so."

PIETRO STEPPED INSIDE THE CAVE. "VITO! IS THIS THE HOME OF VITO the Vituperative? I am Pietro Begnini. I seek an audience."

He went on like this for about fifteen minutes, until at last, a small flame appeared deep within the cave. A voice emerged from the darkness. "What do you want?"

"I want to be a poet," Pietro replied.

"Why?"

"It is my destiny. When I was but an infant, I was given the sign of the sonnet."

"That is not an answer. Why do you want to be a poet?"

"It is my dream."

"Still not answering my question. Let me guess. There's a girl involved."

"Well…yes."

"And she will only marry you if you become a successful poet."

"Well…no."

"She won't marry you even if you become a successful poet?"

"She could not wait for me. She married another."

"Then you're off the hook. Forget about poetry. Pursue an honest profession. Sell snake oil. Take to the stage."

"I do not wish to be anything but a poet."

"You're a stubborn one. Have you applied to the Academy?"

"I spent four years at the Academy. I failed my final examination."

"Oh. That's bad." A figure slowly emerged from the shadows. Pietro expected a shaggy, unkempt feral man, but instead he found Vito looking quite dapper. Tailored shirts. Cuff links. A floral pomade. "What did you fail to do?"

"I could not devise an original metaphor."

"Ouch. That's a tough one. Let me guess. The Grand Inquisitor?"

"Yes."

"I thought as much. He makes the other *crudele bastardi* look like saints. He bribed and poisoned his way to the top, you know. Of course, nothing was ever proved." He sighed, glancing at himself in a small handheld mirror. "I am Vito, the one whom you seek. What can I do for you?"

"I was hoping that you, the greatest of all living poets, could give me a metaphor."

Vito's brow wrinkled. "Do you understand the meaning of

'original?' A poet must see what has not been seen before, or see it in a new light."

"Then perhaps you could instruct me."

Vito smoothed the wrinkles in his trousers. "Do you know how many students I've taken since I left the Academy?"

"None?"

"Fewer than none."

"How is it possible to teach fewer than none?"

"There were two supplicants I not only refused to teach, but actually unlearned what little they already knew."

"I will be no trouble."

"Yes, you will."

"I will do whatever I'm asked."

"No, you won't. Trust me."

"This is my d—"

"Don't play the destiny card. You seek to pass an examination that is only offered once and you have already failed. You seek to marry a woman who has already spurned you and married someone else. Your goals are impossible."

"Are we dead?"

"I can't speak for you, but I'm fairly certain I am not."

"Then it is not impossible. Nothing is impossible to the imaginative mind."

"Oh my. Have you been consorting with Leo? Who thinks men could fly? In little machines with mechanical wings. And that's impossible, too."

"Is that not the job of the poet? To inspire men to dream impossible dreams?"

Vito wagged a finger. "You're good, I'll give you that. But here's the thing. I retired to this cave for a reason. To achieve perfection. Which is impossible out in the world, where you get dirt in your coif and your shirt bunches and it's all just too depressing. I'm not leaving my cave."

"Then I'll live here with you."

"You haven't been invited."

"You can't stop me."

This last remark caught Vito by surprise. In that instant, he glimpsed a fraction of Pietro's determination. "Let me ask you a question. You say you failed your final. Were you cheated? I have a great sympathy for those who have been cheated. If you were cheated, I will teach you."

Pietro hesitated.

"Well? Answer! This is the only way you will ever get me to teach you. Were you cheated?"

"'Cheated' is a vague term…"

"You either were cheated or you were not. Which is it?"

Pietro paused still longer, but eventually answered. "I was not cheated."

"You failed."

"Yes. So you will not teach me." He lowered his head and turned to go.

"One question." Pietro stopped. "Why didn't you tell me you had been cheated? I explained it was the only circumstance that would induce me to teach you."

"My mother said I should not tell lies."

Vito nodded. "And as a poet, I value truth above all else. Beauty is truth, you know." He paused. "And because you are an honest man, I will consider teaching you."

His eyes widened. "Thank you, Vito."

"Call me 'Your Vituperativeness.' But there's a condition that must be met. You have to earn this."

"How do I earn the right to study under you?"

"By slaying the dragon."

Pietro felt his knees weaken. "There are no such things as dragons."

"It's a metaphor, son. No wonder you flunked your final. It's about the hero's journey. Kid leaves home, has adventures, slays the dragon, comes back home again. What it means is, if you want to achieve your dream, you have to earn it. I shall require you to perform twelve labors. Impossible deeds. And if you complete them, I will teach you. And when I'm done with you, you'll have more original metaphors than you know what to do with. Metaphors will stream from your mouth with such alacrity that even casual passersby will be amazed. Everyone will be delighted, except your friends and family, who will soon weary of someone who can't simply say what he means. But that is a problem for later. For now, you have a decision to make. Do you accept the challenge? Can you do the impossible? Twelve times?"

AS YOU MAY HAVE ANTICIPATED, PIETRO ACCEPTED THE CHALLENGE, and thus began the fabled *Dodici Fatiche del Poeta Doofus*. Despite the billing, the first six labors were not impossible but were impossibly boring. They all involved housekeeping. Pietro wondered if the teacher he had sought for so long was not so much a poetical genius as a fussbudget who needed his cave cleaned. Dusting, waxing, sweeping. Scrubbing the rock-laden floors. Laundering Vito's frilly tunics, lace handkerchiefs, and other delicates. Preparing Vito's tea. All of which required several trips to the river and back. His prior service as a pirate's valet was easy by comparison. After several weeks, Pietro complained.

"Look, I want to be a poet, not a servant."

Vito looked away from his mirror. "Are you saying this work is beneath you?"

"Frankly, yes."

"Then you need to do it again."

"That's ridiculous."

"That is what you must do if you hope to be tutored by me."

"But if I spend every day fixing your tea, washing your clothes, cleaning the cave, I will never have time for poetry. Or anything else. Just traveling to the river and back takes half the day."

"So it does."

"I don't want to do it anymore."

Vito turned his back. "Then you will never be my student. And you will never find an original metaphor. And you will never become—"

"Don't you think I know that?" Pietro raced out of the cave. He knew he was relinquishing his greatest dream, and this troubled him mightily. He passed through many steps while grieving for the death of his hallowed objective. Denial: "I can't believe this man wants me to do the impossible." Anger: "What a stupid man he is to expect me to do the impossible." Bargaining: "Couldn't the stupid man make his chores slightly less impossible?" Depression: "I'm so lost and alone and without Sophia, I cannot possibly do the impossible."

And finally, acceptance. It took Pietro a long time to come up with any acceptance. And that of course is what saved him. Because those who accept the death of their dreams will never obtain them.

During the third month after Pietro began his labors, as he walked to the river to fetch more water for the cleaning and the laundry and the tea and the grooming, he saw an elderly man wearing the distinctive garb of the village of Vinci.

"Leo!" he cried, and ran to the man's side—only to find it was not Leo at all but another man assiduously spewing the contents of his stomach into the river. This was not the wild painter and inventor Pietro had come to love but a spice merchant named Raphael whose saffron was poisoned by a Venetian troubadour hell-bent for revenge because Raphael said his singing resembled the howling of she-wolves after they have been wounded. That stung not only because the troubadour prided himself on his dulcet tones but also because he was raised by she-wolves and did not appreciate stereotypical slurs about his family—but that is a story for another day.

Inhaling the fumes rising from the spewage of the old man's stomach made Pietro queasy. He fell to his knees, still with the image of Leo in his head, and recalled the last time he knelt with Leo at the side of a river.

Nothing is impossible…

Very well, Pietro thought. It is time I applied Leo's methods. What is the problem to be solved?

Cleaning the cave requires water.

Fixing Vito's tea requires water.

Laundering Vito's tights requires water.

He perceived a common thread.

He constructed a rudimentary pump, using kinetic energy and the other tricks he'd learned. He wanted to consult with Leo, but he was mindful that Vito told him his labors must be completed without assistance, so he worked from memory. At first, he had difficulty designing the moving parts. The first pump took him a week to construct, and then only worked sporadically. But his work improved with time. Once he had learned to create functional pumps, he went to work on a pipeline. It took him two weeks to create a foot-long piece of pipe from shards of baked earthenware. But the next piece took less time. And the next took less, and less, and eventually the pipeline stretched all the way from the river to the cave. He created a permanent means of bringing water to Vito. As a result, the chores that had previously taken all day now took barely an hour.

"Okay," Pietro told Vito, when at last the pipeline was complete. "Maybe the labors were possible."

Vito nodded. "What have you learned?"

"I know. Nothing is impossible."

"More than that.

"Try, try again?"

"Still more. Initially you were full of anger and arrogance, which made it impossible for you to solve the problem. But eventually, because I pushed, you found a new level of resourcefulness that the cocksure kid who took his final exam did not have. And perhaps more importantly, you learned humility. An essential quality for any poet."

"Are you suggesting that I had a bloated opinion of myself?"

Vito smoothed the lie of his silky hair. "Humility does not mean thinking less of yourself. It means thinking of yourself less."

"Oh, thank you, wise and wonderful Vito."

"Call me 'Your Vituperativeness.' And get some sleep. Tomorrow you begin your seventh labor."

Eighteen

"Surely there will not be six more of these," I said to Giannotti. "He finished all the labors, he received tutoring from Vito, he came up with an original metaphor, he became a famous poet. Along the way, he learned to be trustworthy, loyal, brave, clean, reverent..."

"Not precisely. Remember, Pietro had always been a good boy, so much so that he was loved and cherished throughout Florence. But what Vito immediately perceived was that a poet, a top-flight world-class poet, must be more than simply good. He must have a heart as wide as the Arno. His feelings must run as deep as the Marianas Trench. His character must stand as tall as Everest."

"You could use some tutelage on original metaphors yourself."

"I am but a humble storyteller, not a poet."

"So I'm going to have to listen to the whole catalog of labors?"

Giannotti looked at me sharply. "Do you have somewhere else to go?"

❧

THE SEVENTH LABOR REQUIRED PIETRO TO JOURNEY TO THE neighboring village of Chianti. There he was required to spend a year at a soup kitchen feeding the poor and homeless. When I say "soup kitchen," I employ a modern term to describe an ancient institution. The place where Pietro worked was a gruel kitchen. All they ever served was gruel. Night and day, always gruel. After a few weeks of this, Pietro saw gruel in his dreams, felt gruel beneath his fingernails, smelled gruel in his clothing. But he persevered for the entire year, and by the end of his time there, he had made many friends, not only amongst the staff but also the customers.

"So," Pietro said to Vito, when it was finally over, "I suppose this labor was designed to teach me the virtue of charity. Because poets must possess all the virtues."

Vito removed a speck of lint from his tights. "Certainly poets must understand the virtues, so they can extol them in verse. But must a poet possess them? History would suggest otherwise."

"Then what was the point of this exercise?"

"The point was learning not charity, but compassion. A poet can live without charity, if necessary. But not without compassion. If he has no empathy for the trials of others, his poetry will be empty and meaningless. If he has never felt another's pain, how can he write about it? If he does not know what dwells in the hearts of humans, how can he portray it? Poetry must touch our inner core. It must bring to light what we already knew but had not expressed in words."

"Wow," Pietro said. "If the lesson is that important, this must count as four or five labors."

"Nice try," Vito replied. "But no."

For his next labor, Pietro was required to obtain the girdle of Hippolini, a man in Trieste who favored women's clothing of an Amazonian size. The girdle was crafted from molten gold and was considered one of the greatest metalworking *objects d'art*. Pietro spent several months with Hippolini, delighting him with poetry and his knowledge of rhetorical devices, but the man would not relinquish the valuable belt. Pietro could not buy, beg, or borrow the girdle.

Until he recalled what he had learned from one of Leo's friends. Erasmus taught him that everyone else in the world is not just like you. To understand them, you must put yourself in their shoes and learn what is important to them. So Pietro contemplated. Why does Hippolini treasure this girdle?

Next time he saw Hippolini, Pietro mentioned in passing that he thought the girdle made the man look fat.

"Really?"

"Besides, girdles are passé."

"What's this?"

"Turth." He raised his eyes. "Girdles are so 1470."

The girdle quickly became Pietro's. Afterward, Vito explained that he had hoped the aspiring poet would learn the virtue of tolerance and the importance of empathy, of being able to see the world from a different viewpoint, another essential attribute for a poet.

Labor Nine involved slaying wild beasts, which in this case were two rather scruffy theater agents from Milan. Being a poet, Pietro wasn't willing to slay anyone in the conventional sense, so he decided to slay them with laughter. He wrote a play involving the exploits of a soldier of fortune in a border war who refuses to fight, then convinces his fellow soldiers to join his resistance, denouncing the propagandist rhetoric that started the war in the first place. Eventually the notion spreads to the soldiers on the other side of the border and the governments have no one left to fight for them. By the end of the play, the war is canceled due to lack of interest.

The theatre agents found the play droll if naive and haggled for the right to produce it. They wanted twenty percent of the gross, plus foreign and subsidiary rights and partial ownership of the lead character.

"But," Pietro said, "as patrons of the arts, I thought you would be willing to produce this play without charge as a cultural contribution, as a means of spreading the play's message to those who need to hear it, to enlighten people and spread joy and merriment throughout the land."

That was when he slayed them.

Vito explained that he had assigned this labor because creativity was an essential trait for an aspiring poet. He also noted that although Pietro's play was clever, it was essentially an inversion of *Lysistrata*, a role reversal of *Antigone*, and derivative of the antiwar plays of Cleon. In other words—not original.

The tenth labor required Pietro to seize the Golden Hind of Shebaba, the Woman Who Walks Funny, and the less said about that the better.

While in Bisceglie seizing the Hind, Pietro took time to visit its famed garden. He spent several long hours lost amidst the alpine pansies, the spring pasque flower, and the golden crocus. Just after sunset, as he prepared to depart, he heard a voice coming from somewhere behind him, deep within the forest of fig trees.

"Is it my dear long-lost poet? Pietro?"

He looked up to see a beautiful woman, so filled with grace she seemed to float above the shrubbery. She was older than when he had seen her last, but if anything, even more mesmerizing. Her hair was still as golden as the sun and her skin still as white as the clouds. Her hazel eyes seemed to shimmer.

"Lucy?"

She threw her arms around him. "My poor dear lonely poet."

"I am still not a poet," he said. "But I am working on it."

"What brings you to Bisceglie?"

"I am on an epic quest to complete twelve labors."

"And when you finish, will you be a poet?"

"No, but then I can receive poetical training from a great master. What have you been doing all these years?"

Her eyes drifted to the grass. "I've married twice, never for love. The first was annulled, the second ended in murder. I have a son. And my father is now the Pope."

"Indeed."

"We are very close. But he can be so possessive. I believe he was jealous of my last husband because he was beautiful, while my father's face is ravaged by disease."

"I am sorry you lost your husband."

"He did not love me and I did not love him. I did know love, once, briefly. I met a poet. Perotto. He reminded me of you—so how could I not love him? But my father chased him away and now we are forbidden to see each other or even to write. And thus I am alone again." She brushed his unruly hair from his eyes. "And you, Pietro? Are you still alone?"

"Yes."

"No great beauty has swept you off your feet?"

"As you know, my heart has already been spoken for."

"By the woman who rejected you for another."

"Yes."

She held his shoulders and peered deeply into his eyes. "Such grievous pity for myself I feel/that bliss and agony/give me an equal share of suffering—"

Pietro finished for her, still gazing into her chameleon eyes. "Now that I must, alas, against my will/so sorrowfully breathe/the trembling air of this my final sigh/here in the very heart your lovely eyes wounded…"

She flung her head against his chest. "Pietro, why can we not simply run away together and be happy? Why can't we shake off our past and make a new life together? Why are we denied *la vita nuovo?*"

He felt her trembling. He felt her tears. "I will not say…that I do not believe we could be happy together." He lifted her chin with his finger. "But you have obligations of church and state. And I must finish my quest."

She clutched him all the tighter. "Must it always be so? When may we be happy?"

"Perhaps we are meant for greater things."

She brushed her tears away, still clinging tightly to him. "Will you at least promise me one thing?"

"If I can."

"Will you promise that one day, when we are both old and gray, when my father is dead and can no longer control me, when you either are or are not a poet but either way still deserve to be happy—will you run away with me then?"

He touched her fragile, alabaster cheek. "Perhaps. When we are old and gray."

She smiled a little. "Thank you for at least giving me that."

Nineteen

For the eleventh labor, Pietro was required to clean the Anghiarian stables. At first, he considered diverting the waters of the nearest river with one of Leo's pipelines. Then he learned that this was not simply another cleaning job. The Angharian stables kept cattle for slaughter. The owner wanted the stables cleaned of life.

"I am a poet," Pietro protested. "I cannot be involved in the death of any creatures."

"I'm not asking you to participate in the killing," Vito explained. "The stables are so chaotic that almost a fourth of the cattle die before they arrive for slaughter. They panic, run, stampede. A horrible waste. Your job is one of mercy. Make their final days less traumatic."

Pietro had misgivings, but his desire to be taught by Vito, and the assurances that this was a mission of mercy, overcame them. After observing the stables for many days, he realized why so many of the cattle died prematurely. There was no orderly procedure. As soon as the gates opened, the cattle, seeing what lay ahead, retreated. They had to be forced through the gates with prods and knives. The inevitable result was a stampede. Many cows were lost. Sometimes workers were injured.

One night, while he dreamt, Pietro remembered a test run they once conducted of Leo's first pipeline system. The valves that thrust the water forward worked perfectly, but four different streams reached the pipes at the same time, creating an overflow and wasting water. Afterward, Leo adjusted the valves so they thrust water forward at staggered intervals, never more than one at the same time. No water was lost.

Pietro spent several months creating an equivalent intermittent flow in the Angharian stables. First, he erected a wall that prevented the cattle from seeing where they were headed before they arrived—so they would have no cause to panic. Then he created four chutes to thin the herd. He constructed gates at the end of each chute, then used kinetic energy to create a hydraulic timepiece that released each gate at timed intervals. Only one cow could advance at a time. No more stampedes. An orderly progression.

"Another lesson in compassion?" Pietro asked Vito, when the labor was completed.

"Design," Vito replied. "Inventiveness, planning, and design. Great poems don't just happen. You take an idea, develop it, plan it, then write it. Creativity and organizational skills, working in tandem. The perfect synthesis."

"ARE YOU TELLING ME," I SAID, INTERRUPTING, "THAT THIS wannabe poet invented the modern slaughterhouse?"

"See?" Giannotti said. "My tale is not only instructive but educational."

"I thought Temple Grandin came up with this idea. Funny I never heard about—"

Giannotti shrugged his shoulders. "As you have no doubt already discerned, we Florentines tend toward modesty."

For Pietro's final labor, Vito required him to journey to the faraway Desert of Accona, also known as the Desert of Death and Other Unpleasantness. Pietro was to enter the desert with no food, no water, nothing but the clothes on his back, and to remain there for forty days. Which Pietro thought an insane idea.

"Why would I want to spend forty days in the desert? Why would anyone?"

"You might be tempted," Vito replied.

"I might be tempted to come home and pour myself a glass of wine."

"No, I mean you might be tempted by an incarnation of evil."

"Vultures? Loan officers? Street performers?"

"No. The source of all evil." Vito's voice dropped. "The dark one."

"Then I may need help. Why don't you come with me?"

"And leave the cave? Don't be preposterous. This is the best of all possible worlds. You are the one who seeks improvement, not I."

"Are you sure this is entirely necessary? Because I prefer more temperate climates. And rainfall."

"If you wish to study with me, you will go to the desert. This is when you'll learn your final lesson, and when you'll be most severely tested. But be forewarned—this labor may kill you."

Pietro did not blink. "If this is the only path to my dream, I will not shy from it."

Pietro left for the desert. It took him half a year just to get there. Then it took him many days to unprovision himself, since he was supposed to enter the desert with nothing but the clothes he wore.

When he entered the Acconan desert, he entered alone.

The heat was unbearably intense. Hunger wracked his body. Thirst made it impossible to think clearly. And on the tenth day, the Evil One appeared.

"THE EVENTS I HAVE JUST RECOUNTED," GIANNOTTI EXPLAINED, "and those soon to come, are known in poetic circles by the collective title 'The Temptations of Pietro.' Some scholars have dismissed this entire sequence of events as mythopoetic nonsense. But the account of these events in the assignment book found in Vito's family tomb is quite detailed. Furthermore, there are scattered references in the memoirs of various distinguished members of fifteenth-century Florentine society that corroborate parts of the narrative."

"Have these references been examined by scholars?" I asked.

Giannotti didn't seem to hear. "The most interesting of these accounts comes from the reminiscences of Catherine de Medici. Pietro is known to have met her during his years as companion to Leo, assumed by most to be Leonardo da Vinci, although a splinter group of cryptohistorians believe him to have been a rival inventor known as Leonardo da Rigatoni, who claimed to have invented noodles, although his claims are not well regarded by Renaissance pastaphiles. Medici recorded her conversation with a poet in residence that took place after Pietro's temptations.

"'I had a dream last night,' Medici reportedly said. 'Someone offered to make my area of influence three times as large as it is now.'

"'Was he dark and narrow-eyed?' Pietro is said to have asked.

"'Indeed.'

"'Did the air seem to be sucked out of your lungs when he spoke?'

"'Yes. Exactly.'

"'Did he ask for ten percent of the profits?'

"'How did you know?'

"'That,' Pietro replied, 'was the Evil One.'"

❦

DESPITE THE DESERT HEAT, PIETRO FELT AN UNCOMMON CHILL AS the Evil One approached. He was dressed in soft, loose-fitting clothing. He wore gold chains around his neck. Smoke rose from his fingertips.

Pietro's sunburned face and watery eyes made concentration difficult. The images before him floated and flickered. His knees trembled. He suddenly realized he was standing at the edge of an incredibly high precipice. The ground below was so distant he could not see it.

"I have an offer for you," the Evil One said, his thin lips curled slightly at the edges.

"I will not listen." Pietro's tongue was thick and he found it difficult to speak. "I will not be tempted."

"All I ask is that you hear what I have to say."

"I will not sell my soul to you, not for any price."

"I will give you what you need to achieve your true destiny."

"I will not accept your gifts. I will reject any offer you make."

"Let me make you an offer you cannot refuse." A black rook suddenly appeared in the palm of his hand. "I propose a contest, poet. Do you play chess?"

"Not well."

"Perfect."

"I don't think so."

"Do you play the violin?"

"No."

"Interested in Helen of Troy?"

"No."

"I guess I shall have to try something different this time. Bowling?"

"No."

"Bocce?"

"None of your games will tempt me to sport with you."

The Evil One pondered a moment. "How about a game of rhymes?"

Pietro's sweaty brow creased. "How would long would this take?"

"Until one of us stumps the other. If I win, you listen to my modest proposal."

"And if I defeat you?"

"This will be a much shorter story. But you won't."

"But if I do?"

"I'll go away and leave you to your desert fun. All right?" The Evil One cleared his throat. "The word is 'convey.' Masculine rhyme."

"Dismay," Pietro replied. "Two syllables is too easy. Try three. 'Innundate.'"

"'Calculate.' Four syllables. 'Phenomena.'"

"'Harmonica.'"

"Not bad," the Evil One murmured. "Let us try feminine rhyme. 'Never.'"

"'Forever.' Three syllables. 'National.'"

"'Rational.' For a non-poet, you are most resilient. You may best me at this game. Identity rhyme. 'Motion.'"

"'Promotion.' Three syllables. 'Bookbinder.'"

"'Clockwinder.' Dare we try four? 'Nomenclature.'"

"'Legislature.'"

"Outstanding!" the Evil One enthused. "I don't know how much more of this I can endure. My brain is already taxed. Let's try assonance. 'Home.'"

Pietro realized he was enjoying this. He had always loved the sounds of poetry, and this was a pleasant respite from the boredom of the desert. "'Alone.'"

"Switch to consonance. 'Buddy.'"

"'Body.'"

"Brilliant! Should I even attempt perfect rhymes with one so clever as you? I think I shall. Perfect rhymes. 'Pulchritude.'"

"'Ballyhooed.'"

"'Phosphorescent.'"

Pietro practically sang his reply. "'Incandescent.'"

"'Unanimity.'"

"'Suitability!'"

"'Silver."

Pietro froze. "'Silver—"

The Evil One's eyebrows danced. "Yes?"

"'Silver—"

The Evil One pressed his hands together. "Is there a problem?"

"Nothing rhymes with 'silver!'"

"I accept your resignation. And now you must listen to my proposal."

"THAT'S NOT FAIR," I PROTESTED. "THE EVIL ONE POSED A question that has no answer."

Giannotti nodded. "A tactic employed by politicians and philosophers since the dawn of time. Did you not see it coming? He was building to it for a long while."

"But Pietro should not be beaten with an impossible challenge. He has made no mistake. He has committed no sin."

"The sin was hubris," Giannotti said quietly. "The mistake was accepting the challenge."

"THIS IS MY PROPOSAL," THE EVIL ONE EXPLAINED. "SIGN WITH ME. I'll take you places. I'll make you big. The most famous poet this country ever seen. Bigger than Alighieri. Bigger than Petrarch."

"I do not seek to be the biggest. I simply wish to do the best work I can."

"I'm talking serious money here. I can get you palace bookings, church gigs. Warm-up act at the best hangings. All I want is ten percent of the gross up front. Maybe a cut of the back end, if proceeds exceed expectations or you make it onto the list. Course I'll control media and foreign rights, but we can work that out later. What do you say? Ready to sign?"

"In blood?"

"Don't be primitive. All I need is a handshake."

"I must decline."

"Don't you want to be a poet?"

"I cannot be a poet," Pietro said, fighting to maintain his inner calm, "until I devise an original metaphor."

"You need a metaphor? I got dozens of them. How about this: She was a rose among the dung beetles. He was a candle in the cemetery. Adding a courtesan to the Doge's palace was like taking water to Venice. His was a handsome face in a crowd of dung beetles. The poem was a daffodil in a swarm of dung beetles."

"Not bad," Pietro said, "though you seem to have an unhealthy fixation on dung beetles."

"Then use the other ones."

"They are not mine."

"They're original."

"But they are not mine."

"I know how to keep a secret. No one will know."

"I will know."

The Evil One rubbed a finger across his lips. "A hard case, huh? No problem, I can work with that." He scooped sand into his hand and let it trickle through his fingers. "See this? This are the days of your life. Each grain of sand represents twenty-four hours. And if it seems like there aren't that many of them—it's because there aren't. But I can give you more. Many more. Infinitely more."

"I do not seek immortality, except perhaps through my work. Our mortality is what defines us. It's what makes us strive to achieve, to contribute, to excel."

"With more time, you could write more poetry. Devise more metaphors."

"I only need one. The time I have is sufficient if my brain is willing."

The Evil One clapped his hands together. "Okay. You wanna

play hardball, let's play hardball." He grabbed Pietro by the jaw and squeezed. "I can fix this face."

Pietro tried to speak through scrunched lips. "Ws rng wh my fssss?"

"There is no way to put this but plainly," the Evil One said, pushing him away. "You have the face of a doofus."

"A poet does not need to be pretty."

"Pretty people go places."

"A poet should be known for his verse, not his visage."

"Would it be so horrible to have a face that inspired confidence? To have a countenance that did not immediately cause onlookers to think, 'I would not trust that man with my plumbing, much less my poetry?' Must I remind you that in your hometown, people take their poetry very seriously?"

"My mother gave me this face. My mother loves this face. I have no need of any other."

"Your mother believes you are dead. Everyone in Florence believes you are dead. They have forgotten you. But I can change that. I can make you the most talked-about poet in history. I can make you the most beloved man on the face of the earth."

"Love derived from deception is not true love."

"All right then. I guess there's nothing I can do for you." The Evil One shuffled away, tiny sand clouds rising above his feet. "Oh, there is one other thing." He stopped, then slowly turned to face Pietro, his face frozen in a demonic rictus. "I can make Sophia love you."

"I believe she already does."

"Then you are a delusional fool."

"She told me she loved me. I believe her."

"You believe the words of the most manipulative of God's creatures? No wonder you're unhappy. Make no mistake about this, you who would be a poet. I can give you Sophia. I can make her yours, forever and a day."

Pietro felt a twinge in his left eye. "Sophia has married another."

"I can fix that."

"They are bound in holy matrimony."

"I see an early death in Paolo's future."

"He has done nothing to deserve it, beyond an unhealthy fondness for assonance."

"But you want her. Don't you?" He grabbed Pietro by the shoulders and shook him. "*Don't you?*"

Eternities passed before Pietro answered. "Yes."

"Then take her. Be a man. Fight for what you want. Destroy those who come between you and the woman you love!"

"I will not take another man's wife."

"You know she belongs with you. She is the music to your words."

"Be that as it may, she has married another."

"Fine. Let her be your mistress. Your little bit on the side. Take it from me, it's done all the time."

"Would you debase a thing of beauty?"

"Well, of course, I wouldn't," the Evil One said, "but I understand there are those who do."

"I would never denigrate Sophia. She is an angel."

The Evil One made a wet, sputtering noise. "She is not an angel. Believe me, I know from angels. Did that routine myself, once upon a time. Not all it's cracked up to be. You want to see angels?" He pointed down toward the bottomless pit below. "Throw yourself into the abyss, poet. You will not die. A swarm of angels will catch you."

"That's absurd."

"Are you not a poet?"

"I hope to be."

"Are poets not divine? Anointed by God?"

"I believe that some are."

"Then prove it! Prove that you have the conviction of your words. Haven't you heard that action is character? Throw yourself off the cliff and prove your divinity."

"Only words can demonstrate a poet's worth."

The Evil One thrashed and pulled at his hair. "Execrable scrivener! Do you not understand that I am offering you everything your greasy little heart desires? I can give you the world in the blink of an eye."

"You cannot give me anything, because I would always know it came from you, and thus I would reject it. You only have the power to corrupt art, not to make it."

The Evil One threw himself on the ground, rolling in the sand, kicking his heels in the air, bellowing untranslatable epithets. "I curse you! I curse you and your foolish ambitions. I curse you thus: You will never devise an original metaphor. You will never have Sophia. No matter how hard you try and no matter how hard you train. And my curse will not be broken until you are surrounded by the flames of hell. And when the flames of hell consume you, then you will be mine forever." He bashed his head upon the hard rocky ground until it cracked. A foul black ichor oozed out. A bat flew from his skull and disappeared in the midday sun. What was left of the Evil One shriveled up and blew away like so much desert dust.

Pietro triumphed, but the victory was a hollow one, because he could still hear the Evil One's curse in his ears, and he knew those words could never be unspoken. *You will never devise an original metaphor*, he had said. *You will never have Sophia*.

Never.

Twenty

C hiara brought us a small snack tray, for which I was grateful. The night grew late and I needed something to appease my appetite.

"Only an hour till midnight," Chiara informed us as she set down a lovely plate of antipasti. "Christmas will soon be upon us."

"At the rate this story is unfolding," I said, "you may be serving us breakfast."

She shook her head. "I have plans."

"I forgot. Joining your family?"

"No."

"Husband? Boyfriend?"

Her eyes narrowed slightly. "Actually, I'm performing tonight. A Christmas concert at a church not far from here." She hesitated. "You could come, if you wanted."

"Thanks, but I'm not much for concerts. And for some reason, I want to hear how this story ends."

"Pietro's tale soon will be completed," Giannotti assured me. "You have done a yeoman's labor, Chiara. Why don't you rest your feet and join us?"

"Thank you. I will." She sat on the loveseat beside me.

"What am I supposed to do with this story?" I asked. "I mean, it's entertaining, intermittently. But it's just a story."

Gianotti smiled. "Stories have changed the world, my friend."

"I like to think my narrative poems—"

"Perhaps your current difficulty has arisen because you've lost sight of why we tell stories and write poems. Why they are important to us."

I found the locket tucked inside my pant pocket and squeezed it with all my might.

"Or perhaps," Chiara interjected, "he has known this his entire life. And just needs reminding."

"Everyone needs reminding, every now and again, of what truly matters," Giannotti agreed. "Even Pietro. As we shall see."

Pietro returned to the well-appointed cave of Vito the Vituperative. Having completed his labors and learned his lessons and resisted temptation, his poetical tutelage officially began.

Vito started with a relentless emphasis on metaphor. Pietro had a fine, instinctive grasp of the mechanics of poetry. Vito knew he could teach little there and might even be able to learn. So he focused on Pietro's one weakness, that which had prevented him from becoming a full-fledged poet.

"Metaphor is the heart of all poetry," Vito explained. "Indeed, the heart of all literature. We use symbols to represent intangible virtues. We tell stories of far-flung places or impossible events to reflect on our own lives. The Grand Inquisitor wanted you to fail, to be sure, but he was also correct in his assessment of your qualifications. If you cannot create an original metaphor, a new way of perceiving the world, your poetry will be nothing but pretty words. Appealing, but empty. Incapable of inspiring someone to see what they have not seen before."

"Then I will never be a poet," Pietro said solemnly.

"Nonsense. You survived the twelve labors. You simply need a little push. That is not an insurmountable problem."

"It is my Achilles' heel. My tragic flaw."

"Balderdash. Writing is hard. There's no tougher work in the world. Your problem, Pietro, is that you were born so talented that you were never scared, never hungry, never desperate—and this never needed to channel inspiration. Until it was too late."

"I cannot wait any longer for inspiration!"

"Inspiration comes when you need it most. But let us see what we can do to hasten it along." Vito left the cave—quite a sacrifice for him—and led Pietro to the apex of the tallest of the Tuscan hills. He laid a blanket on the ground and instructed Pietro to lie upon it.

"Look up. What do you see?"

"The sky. Oh—I mean—the sky as blue as a robin's egg."

"That's simile, not metaphor. And hardly original. What else do you see?"

"Clouds. Um, clouds as puffy and white as...my mother's laundry on a windy day."

Vito managed to avoid laughing. "Forget simile and metaphor for a moment. Just *see*. What do the clouds look like?"

"They look like...clouds."

"Focus on the shape, Pietro. Do they resemble other shapes you have seen?"

"They still look like clouds."

"When you were a child, did you never gaze at the clouds and find resemblances to earthly things?"

"I knew other children who did such things," Pietro answered. "I was always too busy with my poetry studies."

"Poetry is more than work, although there is a great deal of work involved. Poetry is about opening your heart. Poetry is about allowing yourself to see what is not immediately apparent to those who do not carry poetry in their hearts." He lay down beside Pietro and pointed to a burgeoning cloud formation in the eastern quadrant. "Tell me what you see."

Pietro peered upward. "It is lopsided, bigger on the top than the bottom, distended about forty-five degrees, with an iridescent ribbon of orange-yellow running through the heart—"

"Yes, yes, excellent descriptive powers, also a valuable talent. But what do you *see*?"

"I see a cloud."

"No, no, no. You see a thin tendril that reminds you of an eel in cold water. You see scalloped ridges that remind you of your sainted tutor's lace handkerchief. You see a protuberant bulge that reminds you of your grandmother's nose wart."

"I really don't…"

"You see a crooked crescent that reminds you of your sweet mother's smile."

Pietro stared at the cloud. He followed each line, striving to discern a pattern. He thought of the clouds like stars in a constellation and strove to see the invisible tethers that formed Cassiopeia or Orion's belt—

But he saw nothing.

"I'm sorry," Pietro said quietly. "The metaphor eludes me."

Vito pushed himself to his feet. "Then we will try something else."

Back in the cave, Vito spent the next day pouring his extensive array of inks onto folded sheets of vellum. He swirled the ink around the paper, then folded it in the middle, pressing the two halves together. He let the ink dry overnight. The result was a series of abstract, symmetrical images.

"Now," Vito said, "let's determine whether you see anything in these."

"Wait a minute," I said. "You're describing Rorschach inkblots."

Giannotti shrugged.

"You're telling me Vito the Vituperative invented Rorschach drawings?"

"Who did you think invented them?"

"Oh, I don't know. Maybe Rorschach?"

Giannotti sipped from his drink. "Many an invention of the modern age is actually the rediscovery or repurposing of an invention of the ancients. Gunpowder, batteries, those little cupholders at the end of movie theater armrests..."

"You're saying Rorschach drawings were invented in the fifteenth century."

"Pietro's friends Leonardo and Botticelli were the first to propose the use of ambiguous designs to gain insight into an individual's personality. But in those days, the designs were used for positive purposes, as a tool to stimulate creativity, not as a game designed to invade someone's psyche."

"I'm finding this difficult to believe."

"Then don't take it literally. Think of it as a metaphor."

"Excuse me?"

"Consider the inkblot tests a metaphor for the tutor's inquiry into the poet's soul."

"I have a sneaking suspicion this entire story is a metaphor for your inquiry into my soul."

"What you hear depends upon you, not me."

"If that's true," I posited, "and the interpretation of a metaphor is infinitely variable and uniquely individual, then Pietro's quest for an original metaphor is a fool's errand."

Giannotti held a finger across his lips. "Perhaps. But let's not tell Pietro."

"A bat," Pietro said. "I see a bat."

"Yes, yes." Vito changed the card. "And this one?"

"Two elephants kissing."

Vito sighed. "And this one?"

"Two women playing chess. With butterflies."

Vito tossed down the images in dismay. "Perhaps I am deluding myself."

"I don't understand the problem," Pietro said, although in his heart, he did. "I looked at the blots. I gave you metaphors."

"You gave me obvious metaphors. Everyday, commonplace, hackneyed metaphors."

"Two elephants kissing is hackneyed?"

"Heard it a thousand times."

"It's what first came to mind."

"I do not think that it is. I think it is what you permitted yourself to say. You are repressing your emotions, keeping them bottled up inside, never letting the world know what lies in your heart."

"I want to be a poet, not a performer."

"And yet, what do the two have in common? Both must stir the audience's emotions."

"Readers should forget that I exist. They should be moved by the power of my words."

"How can you stir emotions when you refuse to experience them yourself?"

To that end, Vito instigated a series of emotion lessons. Pietro spent hours atop a tall hill laughing as hard as his ribs could bear. Vito instructed him to laugh from the heart, sometimes for hours at a time. Vito peppered him with jokes, the problem being that Vito's jokes were more likely to make him cringe than laugh.

On other days, they practiced crying. Vito recited the stories of all the Greek tragedies, the problem being that these stories, laced with improbable plot developments and *deus ex machina* resolutions, were more likely to make Pietro laugh than cry. Vito bullied him, belittled him, called him ugly names. He told Pietro he had the brain of an insect, the maturity of an infant, and the face of a doofus. Sadly, since Pietro disagreed with none of this, it did not make him weep. Vito was reduced to pinching and sucker punches to get tears flowing.

Over the course of the next many months, they covered the full gamut of emotions, large and small, subtle and obvious. Joy, sadness, trust, disgust, fear, anger, surprise, anticipation, and a host of others. When Pietro appeared to have mastered those, when he was able to express them and feel them to the depths of his soul, they tried combining them to create more advanced emotions.

Finally, when the training was at last complete, the time came for an examination Vito called the Experiencing Complex Poetic Emotions Final Exam.

"Are you ready?" Vito asked.

"I am."

"Optimism."

Pietro combined his anticipation face and his joy face. His eyes and mouth were round as circles.

"Very good. Submission."

Pietro combined his trust face and his fear face. Applying his Method, he recalled and reconstructed the expression of the dog he had tossed a rock at when he was thirteen.

"Good. And with a touch of remorse as well. Excellent." Vito cleared his throat. "Awe."

Pietro combined fear and surprise, recalling the day he was first brought to the Academy.

"Very good. Contempt."

Pietro combined disgust and anger, reliving the moment in which the Inquisitor told him he had failed the examination.

"Fantastic. And now the final challenge." He paused a moment. "Love."

Pietro did not react. He seemed confused.

"Love," Vito repeated. "You know what it is. We've discussed this."

Pietro's face darted one direction then another. "That is not really a complex emotion."

"Indeed it is. Let me give you a hint. Combine joy and trust."

But Pietro could not do it.

"Concentrate," Vito said. "Remember what I told you. Take a deep breath. Exhale slowly. Release the tension in your shoulders. Close your eyes. Focus on a vibrant moment from your childhood. Expose yourself. Scrutinize your soul. Imagine you are floating. See the world from a distance. Obtain an objective viewpoint. Make your heart obey your instructions. Recall your mother, cradling your infant self in her arms. Recall your father, instructing you on the fundamentals of produce. Recall the first time you heard Sophia sing. What is music but love? What is poetry but love? Capture that love in your heart. Think of the greatest poetry you have ever heard, how it took the top of your head off, how it transported you to another place, another time, other doors, other windows. Find a quiet place within yourself. Dig deeper. Then deeper still. Find the truth that wears a mask. Give me—"

"Please stop," Pietro said. "You're making my head hurt."

"Then show me love."

"I can't!"

"If you don't," Vito said, "then you fail the final examination. Again."

"As indeed I always knew, deep within, that I would."

"Just show me love!"

"The only love I have known, other than my parents', was from Sophia. But I cannot think of her without feeling pain."

"Then show me the pain. Sometimes love hurts. Love can cut like a razor. Show me the razor."

But Pietro could not do it. Even after almost eighteen years, the wound was too fresh and the pain was too intense. "I will write on other subjects," he said at last.

"Other than love? You will be a poet who cannot write about love?"

"Then I will say what has been said before. Only better."

"What do you think we have been working toward? You

cannot go out there writing the same things everyone has heard a hundred times. Critics will rip you to shreds. You will never survive."

"Maybe I will."

"They'll crush you like a grape in a wine stomp."

"You don't believe in me."

"As if you were my own son, I do. But I will not encourage you to do that which I know will be a failure."

"How could you know?"

Vito answered so loudly stalagmites shattered. *"Why do you think I'm in this cave?"*

The silence that followed reverberated almost as much as Vito's words.

"I had wondered..." Pietro ventured.

Vito lowered himself to a boulder. "I was once a student in the Florentine Academy of the Poetical Arts. I was considered the best and the brightest of my generation. At the Christmas Eve recitation of 1469, I received three standing ovations. Luigi—the man you know as the Grand Inquisitor—was the only poet who approached my prowess, but he was generally acknowledged to be my inferior by the Academy cognoscenti. We both passed our final examinations—not to rub it in, but we did—and believed we were destined for great things. The Grand Inquisitor of that time was in failing health and there was much talk about who would be his successor. I was the favored candidate."

Vito's eyes seemed to recede into his head. "Some felt I should be appointed by acclamation, but Luigi understandably objected. He wanted to be considered. A contest was proposed. We would both recite our best work and be judged by a panel of distinguished critics. I should have foreseen what would happen. But I was so full of myself, so confident of my own powers, I did not see what should have been obvious.

"The performance began. I spoke first. I had written nothing new for the occasion, preferring to rely on audience-tested favorites from my years at the Academy. The crowd adored me.

They clapped, they cheered. 'Bravo,' they cried. 'Bravissimo.' Their enthusiasm filled my heart. But if I'd had any sense, I would've watched the expressions on the faces of the critics. Because they were not smiling at all.

"Luigi recited to what I would call polite indifference. The audience was never rude, but they were certainly not enthusiastic. There was scattered applause and the faintest hint of snickering. To me, the result seemed a foregone conclusion."

Vito sighed heavily. "I could not have been more devastatingly incorrect. 'Derivative,' one of the critics said of my work. 'Panders to the hoi polloi.' 'Obvious,' said another. 'Accessible to a fault.' The kindest judge contented himself to say that my work was 'not entirely without merit.' But when it came to Luigi's work, they were adulatory. They trumpeted his originality. They said his work 'invites, nay demands, scholarly analysis.' They said his 'metapoetic excursions redefine the very nature of the verse enterprise.' They chose him, Pietro. They chose *him*.

"I risked everything I had on what I believed to be an inevitable outcome. I spent every cent I had on preparation and costuming. I mortgaged my house, my future. I even risked the woman I loved, regaling her with foolish tales of what her life would be like married to the Grand Inquisitor. But when it was all over, I could not deliver on my promises. She ran away with a Milanese stonemason. I was completely broken. Penniless. And Luigi had my job."

"He must have bribed the critics," Pietro said.

"Yes of course he did, and the ones he could not bribe he poisoned, but that doesn't change the fact that I let it happen. I was sloppy, overconfident. I should've kept my eye on him, and I should have been devising better poetry. But I didn't. After I was defeated, I was so ashamed I ran away and holed up in this cave, hiding from the world that had once been everything to me, trying to restore my ravaged self-image. At first I blamed Luigi, or I blamed the critics. But that was the reaction of a petulant child. Now I realize I had no one to blame but myself."

He glanced upward with moist eyes. "And that is why I must be honest with you, even though it pains me to do so. I cannot allow you, who have already suffered so much, to suffer again. I have tried to teach you. But I have failed. You are not a poet. If you attempt to present yourself as one, it will only end in misery and grief."

"I...understand." Pietro rose, fighting back the complex emotions he felt. "I will abandon this dream. I will think no more of poetry. For the rest of my life."

Twenty-One

Pietro failed his final examination from Vito, the last examination of his life. It had taken him eighteen years, but at long last he accepted the fact that he would never be a poet, that after all his many years of wandering, he would never achieve his dream. He told himself it was simply not meant to be and tried to put it out of his mind.

He returned to Florence where he found much had changed, but really not all so much, except that everyone thought he was dead. At his parents' home he was greeted by his mother who, once she overcame her initial shock, wrapped him in her arms, asking no questions, saying she had missed him and she was glad he was well and by the way you haven't been throwing any more rocks at dogs, have you?

His father was a different story.

Pietro found Sal at his vegetable stand, supplying produce to his loyal customers as he had always done. He too was startled to see Pietro arisen from the dead, but soon recovered himself and listened to Pietro's tales from his many years of journeying.

"The long-lost prodigal poet returns."

Pietro winced. "I am not a poet. I am just Pietro, the same boy I have always been."

"The boy with the seal of the sonnet."

Pietro shook his head. "No more."

"You were gone a long time."

"I needed to learn about the world. To have adventures. To find out who I am meant to be."

"You didn't write. Not once."

"I am sorry. I was preoccupied."

His father busied himself with the turnips, never making eye contact. "So I guess you'll be going back to that Academy?"

"No. I want nothing to do with poetry. Ever again."

His father slowed. "Then how will you occupy yourself?"

"I don't know. I thought perhaps I could…assist you with the vegetables."

"I wouldn't want you to demean yourself. Peddling potatoes and such."

Pietro drew himself up. "I was a young man when I said that. I am young no longer."

His father shrugged. "Could use a little assistance around here. Can't tote the big bags like I once did."

"I could help with that."

"Big discount markets are stealing my customers with drastically reduced prices for vegetables of drastically reduced quality. I can't buy them as cheap as those people sell them."

"Perhaps you should try vertical integration. Grow your own crops."

"I don't know from agriculture."

"I do. Leo made a study of it. There are many scientific advances that could have applications in your line of work. And I could spruce up your image and improve the appearance of your stand."

"So now you're a personal groomer?"

"I learned much about grooming from my teacher Vito. And much about art from Botticelli and much more from many others. Once we have improved this stand, we could expand, forming a chain of stands, one on every bridge in Florence. You could become the King of Florentine Vegetables."

"Did this Vito also teach you about building business empires?"

"No," Pietro replied. "I learned about that from the Evil One."

"Does this mean you will be around more than you have been the last, oh, I don't know, eighteen years or so?" He looked away. "It would mean a lot to your mother."

"I will be around every day till the end of your days. I will be around so much you will wish I would go away occasionally."

His father placed a hand on Pietro's shoulder. "I doubt that."

PIETRO JOINED THE FAMILY BUSINESS, APPLYING EVERYTHING HE HAD learned during his eighteen-year hegira to cultivating and selling vegetables in the Cradle of the Renaissance. He implemented Leo's pump and pipeline system again, this time to water vegetables cheaply and efficiently. His hard-won knowledge from Vito of the import of food cleaning and presentation resulted in the finest vegetables in Florence. He borrowed Buonarrotian motifs to illustrate the storefronts and to create a distinctive corporate logo.

His greatest innovation, however, was the adaptation of Leo's Kongming lanterns to the transport of produce. Pietro built a box-shaped frame from lightweight wood, then covered it with a taffeta cloth and inflated it with hot air from a fire. The balloon rose and travelled along a rope tether from the bank of the Arno, where the vegetables were brought from the farms, to the vegetable stands where they were sold. In time, he created larger balloons with increasingly greater hauling capacities. This reduced their shipping costs significantly while also creating a spectacle that brought pleasure to all of Florence.

Customers loved Pietro. Despite his long absence, most still remembered that he had always been a good boy, and most felt he had gotten a raw deal in that business with Sophia. They shopped at his stands even when they could spend fewer florins elsewhere. Families chose to trade with him. Mothers brought their small children to see him—although it should be noted that they rarely brought their dogs. Soon the Begninis were one of the most prosperous families in Florence. And by all appearances, Pietro was one of the happiest men in Renaissance produce.

But his father had known Pietro for a long time. He was able to see that which others did not.

"You did a good job with the kumquats today, son."

Pietro was taking down the stand for the night. "Thank you, Father."

"I suppose now you'll be off carousing with the boys."

"No, Father."

"Preying on the ladies, eh?" He winked. "We are Florentines, are we not?"

"No, Father. I mean, yes, we're Florentine, but no."

"Son…it's been eighteen years since…"

"Yes?"

Sal exhaled heavily and started over. "Here's the thing, son. I've lived a long time, at least by contemporary standards. But no one gets as much time as they'd like. That's why it's important to make the most of every day. I know you didn't spend the first forty years of your life planning to become a vegetable magnate. Well, fine. You can't always get what you want. But if you try sometimes…you can still live a good happy life filled with love. And that's more than most get."

"Is that what you and Mother have?"

Sal grinned. "We've been together more than forty years, son. When I was a young man, I thought love was about dramatic revelations and fantastic beauty and high romance. All of which is good, but it doesn't last, and it isn't exactly love so much as entertainment. What I've learned over time is—love is in the quiet moments." His father rubbed his eyes. "So get out there, son. Meet people. Find someone."

"No, Father. That part of my life is over. There is no substitute for gazing into the face of an angel."

Although he never inquired, Pietro learned that Paolo had moved to Rome shortly after his marriage. And naturally, he took his new bride with him. They had never returned.

Nonetheless, to all outward appearances, Pietro was happy and content. His aptitude for business far outstripped any other former student of the Florentine Academy of the Poetical Arts. Profits soared.

But every Christmas Eve, Pietro observed poets filing into the churches. And a tiny light in his heart was snuffed out. Over and over again.

He made a point of having nothing whatsoever to do with the Academy, the Guild, or any of the Florentine Poetry Establishment. He did not attend recitations, slams, recitals, fetes, or signings. Even when his friend Machiavelli published the latest volume of his history of Florence, Pietro did not attend. He resolved to let the past be the past. To move forward with his new life as a retailer of calcium-rich comestibles.

One day, the Grand Inquisitor, older now but still active, came by the vegetable stand where Pietro worked. He spoke not a word, but simply observed. He surveyed the banner over the stand. He ran his fingers lightly over the vegetables. And at long last, he looked at Pietro. Looked directly into his eyes.

And smiled.

Pietro did not sleep that night. But the next day, he was back at the farm, back at the stand, doing the work he had agreed to do.

In that particular year, the annual Calcio Storico Fiorentino was held at the winter solstice, not during the summer as it is today. This sporting match, the final game of the season for an early precursor of rugby, celebrates the perseverance of those who endured the Florentine Siege, when papal troops surrounded the city but sport continued in defiance and contempt of the encircling enemy. In Pietro's day, this annual recreation was considered the first event in the celebration of the Christmas Feast Week.

Florence took its Calcio Storico very seriously. Not as seriously as its poetry, of course. What civilized society ever considered sport more important than poetry? Still, it was a major civic event, attended by virtually everyone, and there is no greater proof of its import than the fact that the major poets of the day were always asked to recite at halftime.

In fact, this year, the city invited the greatest poets of the Class of '81—Pietro's class—to return to their homeland and recite. That, of course, would include Paolo, son of the vintner, now apparently thriving in Rome. And that was important.

Because if Paolo returned at long last to Florence, Sophia was sure to accompany him.

Twenty-Two

"About time," I said. "This story has been without romance for too long."

"Ah," Chiara said, still sitting beside me. "So the poet has a taste for love."

"It helps a story go down."

"You do not fool me. May I ask you a question? Why is one so romantic all alone?"

"What makes you think I'm alone?"

"You have occupied your room without company for seven months. There is no ring on your finger. And you are spending Christmas Eve listening to my employer tell a long story."

"I think I mentioned earlier that I ended a relationship shortly before I came to Florence. I needed to focus on my work. Without distractions."

"And how is that working out?"

I mumbled a nonresponse.

"It is not easy for you," she asked, "is it? Meeting people."

"I get...awkward."

"As a child, you had many sisters, but no brothers."

I avoided her gaze. "Yes..."

"Did you stammer?"

"And had a speech impediment."

"Glasses?"

"Big thick ones."

"Athletic?"

"Scrawny."

"Picked on by bullies?"

"Constantly."

"You felt isolated. Alone."

"Are you asking me or telling me?"

"Your father criticized you constantly. Perhaps even struck you."

"Why do I feel like I should be lying down?"

Giannotti chuckled. "You must forgive Chiara. She is quite the detective. I told her she should study psychology, but she insists on pursuing music. Managing the Palazzo to support herself while she composes her masterpiece."

"I am sorry," Chiara said. "I get interested and I do not know when to stop." She squeezed my hand. "I did not mean to make you uncomfortable."

I felt a shiver race up my spine. Apparently the night was growing cold. "I know we're getting close to midnight, Giannotti, and I don't want Chiara to miss the ending. So perhaps we should proceed."

Giannotti nodded. "As you wish."

On the day before Christmas Eve, virtually everyone in Florence gathered at the Tontino, the city's largest open air auditorium. For the sports aficionado, of course, the Calcio Storico was the game of games. But for many, the highlight was the half-time show, with its headliner-poet recitals. This year, the Grand Inquisitor himself, long absent from public readings, consented to share his most recent work. This created an irresistible draw.

But Pietro wanted nothing to do with poetry readings, the

Grand Inquisitor, or any forum in which Paolo and his lovely bride were likely to be present. He told his father he would watch the vegetable stand. Even though he was sure to have no customers.

I should say a few words about the Grand Inquisitor, lest he come across as a cardboard villain. His road to the Inquisitorship was a long and difficult one, and his past in many respects explains why he behaved as he did, and why he committed the horrible deed I am about to—

"No!" I said abruptly. "Don't do it!"

Giannotti sat up. "What is it you think I am going to do?"

"The worst of all storytelling crimes. Dumping exposition. You're about to sidetrack the story—just as it approaches the climax—with a lot of backstory that doesn't advance the narrative. You're going to tell us the Inquisitor had a troubled childhood or his mother didn't hold him enough or some other trite explanation for why he's such a crudele bastardo."

"But it's true."

"I don't care. It's bad writing. And besides, it's too late for that sort of thing. Get on with the tale."

Giannotti thrust his hands into his pockets. "This is the way I have always told it."

"Then you're overdue for revision."

As I said, the entire city descended upon the Tontino for the match, except Pietro.

The Inquisitor had a special stake in this halftime reading. The reappearance of Pietro, even as a vegetable merchant, spawned a deep-seated need to prove he was still the premiere poet-in-residence, probably the result of insecurities that went back to—

"You're doing it again!" I said, pointing an accusatory finger. "This is an infodump."

"Just be quiet and listen," Giannotti snapped.

What no one in Florence at that time realized was that the Inquisitor—his real name was Luigi Andretti—was not only Vito's former rival but also Vito's half-brother. Vito was his father's official son by his official wife. Luigi was the child of a mistress he kept in a third-rate shack on the wrong side of the Arno. Vito was raised to a life of privilege and wealth. Luigi never had enough of anything, especially his father's attention. Vito went to private schools, wore the best clothes, always had money for gelato and biscotti. Luigi went to public school, wore shabby clothes, and never had any money at all. Vito was handsome, athletic, and popular. Luigi had a sour expression, spindly legs, and was widely disliked. You see the problem.

Their father was a tradesman, but his great love was poetry, so both boys set their sights upon a career in the poetical arts. Vito appeared to have all the advantages. He was smart, quick, and frankly, a better poet. Vito was ranked 1st among living poets, while Luigi was merely 2nd. Luigi resented this. To him, Vito was a trust-fund poet, a silver-spoon upstart. He made it his life's mission to bring Vito down. To prove to the Guild that he was the superior poet. To prove to his father that he was the better son and the one who deserved his affection. So he sabotaged Vito and cheated him out of the Inquisitorship. Even long after their father passed away, Luigi was determined to demonstrate at every possible opportunity that he was the greatest living poet.

You must understand that at the time of the Calcio Storico, the Inquisitor had recently had a birthday. He was now fifty-nine, which of course meant that he was over-the-hill, especially by the standards of Renaissance Italy, where the average life expectancy was thirty-eight. He knew his poetic powers were waning. So what he could no longer accomplish with words, he was determined to accomplish with spectacle—not the first nor the last artist who would make such a substitution. If his part of the halftime show was lacking in content, he would compensate with special effects.

During a sojourn to Cathay, the Inquisitor had learned the ins and outs of gunpowder and fireworks. He planned to put on the greatest pyrotechnic show Florence had ever seen.

Unfortunately, his need to assert his preeminence caused him to pay more attention to the spectacle than the safety procedures...

The sporting match was first-rate, just close enough to be engaging without putting anyone in serious doubt as to the outcome. The home team led all the way, but only by a few points and with great effort. The Florentine goalie made a spectacular head-first dive to block a kick that would have permitted the Roman opposition to take the lead in the final minute before halftime. Thrilling.

To kick off the halftime ceremonies, the Duke announced the names of the young women chosen to serve as this year's homecoming poetry princess and her attendants. A succession of the best and brightest Academy students escorted them across the field to thunderous applause. And then at long last it was time for the poetry readings.

The stage jutted out from the retaining wall at the south end of the Tontino. One by one, the poets mounted the stage and presented their work. The city's currently ranked fourth-best poet was unable to attend for reasons of health. But the third- and second-ranked poets read commemorative poems composed for the occasion. The second-ranked poet was Pietro's old school chum Georgio who, while Pietro was on the road for eighteen years, had an exciting career as a crusader, spy, monk, and for a brief time, the dread highwayman Piranchellus—but that is a story for another day.

After Georgio finished, the Grand Inquisitor rose. He mounted the stage in his flowing black robes, arms spread wide, and just as it looked as if he were about to speak—multi-colored explosions illuminated the open-air auditorium. The crowd gasped. Most had never seen fireworks and none had seen a display so spectacular. Huge floral patterns crisscrossed the night sky. Starbursts of color flooded the field of vision. Some believed the lights formed constellations illustrating the themes of the Inquisitor's poetry.

But there was one problem—the rocket that was supposed to speed upward to unprecedented heights for the grand finale. What the Inquisitor had not taken into account was the extraordinary confluence of winds crisscrossing Florence that night. Normally, the wind blew north off the Mediterranean, providing the gentle caressing breezes so beloved by citizens and tourists alike. On this rare day, a contrapuntal wind blew south, straight off the arctic, cold and harsh. Meteorologists of the time had never seen anything like it. It is still considered an unprece- dented extreme-weather phenomenon. But the point is, after the rocket launched, it slammed against a southerly wall of wind, pivoted, and descended from whence it had come. Into the heart of the Tontino.

This auditorium, when not used for civic assemblies, was made available to artists and artisans who could not afford their own studios. That meant the wooden building was filled with paint, turpentine, and oil-soaked rags. In other words, the only items that could be more flammable than the auditorium were the contents of the auditorium. When the rocket hit, the building erupted into flames.

Florence, the jewel of the Renaissance, was on fire. In a matter of seconds, flames surrounded the stage, trapping the performers within. Snaking tendrils of fire leapt toward the seats, threatening all those present. The city, its people, its poets, their families, and the greatest art treasures ever known to man, were all in danger.

Including the visiting poet Paolo.

And his wife.

Twenty-Three

Y ou may recall that the only person not attending the match and consequently not immediately threatened was Pietro. You may be expecting him to save the day. Alas, Pietro was understandably feeling despondent, given the knowledge that Sophia must be very near, so he took a strong sleeping draught and went to bed early. He slept through the explosion.

The rocket had ignited the Tontino. The impact was thunderous, shaking the aged building and its occupants. One person tumbled into another, unable to maintain balance. People panicked, screamed, pushed, shoved. Where once had been the beauty and majesty of poetry, now was only the terror of those who knew they were about to die.

Paolo and Georgio and the other poets trapped by flames scrambled for a way out, but the wall of fire was too thick, too tall, too hot. There was no escape. The flames crept forward, pressing them closer and closer to the wooden wall that backed the stage. A wooden stile used by the stage crew was too high to reach. The wall itself was too smooth and steep to climb.

Many of the trapped poets lost their nerve. They ran one direction then the other. The heat seared their faces. The smoke choked them. Black clouds billowed, making it almost impossible to breathe. Each was struck with the unshakable certainty that they faced imminent death.

The fierce wind continued to blow, hurling fireballs about the stage. The turmoil of frenzied desperate bodies soon made forward passage impossible. You know what happens when someone yells "Fire!" in a crowded theater? Well, that was exactly what happened here except more so, because everyone was yelling "Fire!" because there really was one.

The Tontino had become a cauldron of death.

In the midst of the horror, a sure sign of the heroism and fiber of the Florentines is the fact that some scattered individuals managed to keep their wits about them. One poet named Yusef attempted to scale the back wall. Enlisting help from a few friends, he freed a long wooden bench, the seating for an entire row of spectators. Fighting against the dense smoke and soot, they hoisted the heavy bench upright and propped it against the wall vertically, hoping to create a makeshift ladder. Yusef stood at the base while another man climbed atop his shoulders, then another on his, clinging to the bench. But when they reached the top, they saw what had previously been shrouded by smoke. The bench was at least ten feet short of the top of the wall. They tried to extend the human ladder, just standing on one another's shoulders with nothing to grip, but their balance was too precarious. The human ladder collapsed. They tumbled to the ground.

Georgio proposed removing their poet robes and flapping them to extinguish the flames. Removing even a single layer of clothing, when the inferno was so near, required enormous courage, but he did it. Unfortunately, the air currents he created were no match for the titanic southerly wind. Others joined in but it made no difference. In fact, the flames seemed to rise taller and creep closer. By the time the flapping was done, the ring of fire barely measured eighty feet in diameter.

One by one, the poets fell to their knees and addressed prayers to Columba. They did not pray for safe deliverance, because even the dullest among them could see that was no longer possible. Instead, they prayed for safe passage to the land of heavenly peace and everlasting verse.

There was one poet who made no attempt to escape—because he was not there. Alone amongst his poetic brethren, the Grand Inquisitor had escaped. Because he knew that his rocket had gone wrong even before it struck the auditorium, he was able to react more rapidly than most. In his cowardly panic, he saved himself—but no one else.

For many years, the Inquisitor's means of egress from the inferno was unknown. We had no clues until certain excavations in the latter half of the twentieth century at the location of the former auditorium yielded traces of what some believe to be an underground passageway. Why would the Tontino have a secret tunnel? Some hypothesize that it may have been a storage place for forbidden spirits. Some believe it was a trysting place for the Grand Inquisitor and his groupies. Whatever the reason, no one seemed to know about the tunnel but the Inquisitor. So while others fought valiantly but futilely against certain death, the Inquisitor sneaked away.

And while this hellish scenario threatened the people, architecture, and treasures of Florence, Pietro slept.

"Pietro slept?" I could barely contain myself. "He *slept*?"

Giannotti nodded.

"He's the hero of this story."

"Indeed."

"The hero can't sleep while the city burns. While his true love is incinerated."

"I am only telling you what happened."

"You're telling a story. And forgive me for saying so, but at the moment, the story stinks!"

"Love does not always triumph." Giannotti paused. "I would think that you of all people would know that."

I took a deep breath and gathered my thoughts. "People love stories because they're better than reality."

Giannotti shook his head. "People love stories because they show us the truth."

WHAT YOU MUST UNDERSTAND BEFORE WE PROCEED ANY FURTHER IS that poets do not sleep like other people sleep. When you sleep, perhaps you dream of the ones you love. Or perhaps you are tormented by past sins, premonitions of future dangers, monsters lurking within your own psyche. But when the best and brightest poets sleep, they see words. Language comes to them, felicitous turns of phrases, expressions that make the difference between a passable poem and a work of genius. This was never more true than with Pietro, because during his waking hours, he did not allow himself to think of poetry at all. He repressed that which was most fundamental to his being. So of course, as all good Freudians must have already realized, poetry emerged with brutal violence during his slumber.

I probably do not need to tell you that poetry is by its nature empathic. This was something Vito tried to impress upon Pietro back in the cave. Some people have wondered whether extrasensory perception exists and have conducted scientific experiments to prove or disprove it. They would have been wiser to read poetry. The very nature of poetry puts the reader in touch with the feelings of others. Why else would poetry move us to laughter or to tears? Why did the groundlings cheer when Henry V rallied his troops? Why do we feel such sorrow at the deaths of the cavalrymen of the Light Brigade? How can we so viscerally experience the loss of Annabel Lee? Because that's what poetry does. So how could Pietro not feel the fear and panic experienced by so many so nearby?

Pietro awoke with a start.

"Someone is in danger," he murmured.

He blinked. He smelled smoke. He perceived fear.

"My parents are in trouble." And then, barely a second later, he added, "Sophia."

He was out of the house running in barely a second, tearing down the streets of Florence. He ran in his nightshirt and stocking feet, moving as quickly as he could. He needed no directions. The burning amphitheater was visible throughout the city. Smoke clouds billowed like a beacon overhead.

Less than a minute later he was at the scene. He stopped and pressed his nightshirt against his nose and mouth, struggling to breathe.

The tumultuous noise made it difficult to think. People screamed, shouted, cried. Chaos reigned. A fortunate few had managed to escape the Tontino, but not many. The fire had weakened overhead girders, blocking two of the three exits. One remained passable, but so crowded with human bodies that traffic slowed to a near standstill. At this rate, most would burn or be trampled before they could flee.

Pietro understood the situation immediately. The city of Florence was on the brink of extinction. If something didn't happen quickly—everyone and everything he loved best was doomed.

Twenty-Four

Pietro gaped at the burning auditorium. The heat was so intense he could feel it on his face, even from a distance. He could only imagine what the people inside must be suffering. Like his mother. Like Sophia.

"They must escape," he said, thinking aloud, "but this frenzied madness makes that impossible. They need to take turns. To move in an orderly fashion."

Something snapped inside Pietro's head. He had done this before.

He looked around, searching for the highest possible perch. A nearby campanile stood only a few feet from the auditorium. He raced to it. The door was locked. He threw himself against it with all his might. The door barely budged. He hammered the door again and again until it yielded.

Pumping hard with thighs hardened by months of trudging through the desert, he flew up the stairs until he reached the highest level. He threw open the double doors and stepped onto the balcony. From this elevated perch, he could see exactly what was happening in the auditorium.

The only exit not in flames was clogged by debris and human bodies struggling to get out. Four streams of people moved toward it, one from each level and direction. They all pushed hard, terrified by the encroaching flames. The inevitable result was that no one went anywhere.

The ring of fire surrounding the stage had grown so tall Pietro could not tell what was happening within. His friends, the greatest poets of Florence and their families, were trapped.

He turned his attention back to the exit. First he had to clear out as many spectators as possible. Fortunately, he had relevant experience. Because as much as he loved these people, at this moment, they were no different from the cattle in the Aligherian stable that panicked when they realized they were being led to the slaughter. He had to calm them down. And he had to do it fast.

He had no megaphone, the acoustics were poor, the flames were loud, and the crowd was even louder. Commanding their attention and trust seemed impossible—especially for him. But in the darkness, no one would see the face of the doofus. They would only hear the voice like an angel.

"L—L—L—" He found himself stuttering like he had not stuttered since the first time he tried to speak to Sophia. He steeled himself, dredged up the courage he needed.

"Listen to me!" he shouted. His first words made no impression on the madding crowd. He said it again and again, increasing his volume each time. He inhaled deeply, tightened his diaphragm, and spoke with such power that it is said they could hear it on the other side of the Arno. "Listen to me!"

There was the tiniest slowing, quieting, inside the auditorium.

"I can help you!" Pietro bellowed. "Let me help you!"

Somewhere deep within the auditorium, someone spoke. "I know that voice. It is…the vegetable vendor."

"Listen to me!" Pietro shouted. "I can get you out of there!"

The tumult subsided, though the pushing and shoving did not. "You have two choices. You can continue fighting as you are now, in which case no one will survive. Or you can take turns. I can help you do that. And you will all live. What do you choose?"

The response was muffled and confused, with many people talking at once.

Okay, Pietro told himself, there are four streams, four cattle chutes, so to speak. They must be opened in rotation. If too many people see the exit at once, they will bolt and the passage will be blocked again.

"Those of you on the ground floor, coming in east of the exit. Do you hear me?"

Enough people waved their hands that Pietro could tell some had heard and some knew which direction was east. He identified each of the other three streams in the same manner.

"I'm going to ask you to do something hard," he shouted. "This may be the hardest thing you have ever done. I'm going to ask you to stop pushing. All of you. Stand still. Don't shove. Don't strain."

Not much changed.

"Do you want to get out of there? The fire grows by the second. You cannot continue doing that which has been unsuccessful repeatedly and expect a different result. That is madness. If you want out, listen to me. Stop pushing!"

Even from his high perch, even in the darkness, Pietro could see that the tension in the tightly packed crowd slowly eased. People nudged one another, pointing toward the voice in the campanile.

"Now we're going to take turns." The flames must have a reached a new storage place filled with combustibles, because all at once they heard a booming explosion and more flames shot skyward. People screamed. The pushing and shoving restarted as everyone desperately tried to escape.

The sudden flare also allowed Pietro to see more clearly. "Okay, you on the left. Joseph, the fisherman, and your wife. I want you to step forward. No one else! Just you two." The crowd eased enough to let them pass. "Excellent. Now on the upper left. "Timothy, the bookbinder. Take your daughter and move toward the exit. Don't worry. They'll let you pass."

"Me next!" some cried, or "I have to get out now!" but Pietro remained calm and kept to his plan. Slowly he worked his way through the crowd, to the upper west, then ground west. Then he started over again, working through the four streams of people just as he had done with the cattle, except this time, instead of leading creatures to their death, he led them to their salvation. In less than ten minutes, he had all the spectators out of the burning auditorium. Brother hugged brother and couples shouted for joy, delirious at being released from what had seemed a certain incineration.

Many raced for the safety of their homes, especially those who had trouble breathing in the dense smoke. But many of the strongest breathers remained because they knew not everyone was safe. The poets remained trapped within the ring of fire circling the stage. And no voice from the heavens, no orderly procedure, could save them.

Pietro thought as hard as he could but no solution came. The only source of water, the Arno, was too far away. The fireboats had hoses, but they were not long or strong enough to reach the auditorium. The wind fanned the flames, nurturing them, not diminishing them. There was no likelihood of rain. Saving the poets, he thought, is impossible.

He heard an old friend's voice echoing inside his head. "Are we dead?"

Net yet, Pietro murmured.

Then it is not impossible.

Think!

Pietro raced down the stairs to join those he had saved, racking his brain all the while.

At just that moment, the Grand Inquisitor emerged from the shadows. Pietro almost collided with him on his way out of the campanile.

"Inquisitor! Does this mean the poets have been saved?"

"Uh, no," he said, coughing for dramatic effect. "I was separated from the other poets after the initial blast. I joined those in the stands and managed to escape when they did."

"We have to get the poets out!"

"Alas, it cannot be done. I searched thoroughly, putting my own life at great risk, but there is no passageway. I fear they are lost."

"I do not accept your fatalistic conclusion," Pietro said.

"That was your problem at the Academy," the Inquisitor replied. "One of them, anyway. You were trained to accept the no-win scenario, to let it teach you humility. But instead of accepting it, you cheated your way around it."

"And I still reject it," Pietro said. "There is always a solution. To any problem. For the imaginative mind."

"Then what is it, imaginative one?"

"We need to bring water to the auditorium. Much water."

"Obviously. But that cannot be done in time. Stop wasting your breath and do something useful. Begin your prayers for the dead."

Pietro closed his eyes and thought as hard as he could. He thought with such intensity that in later years many of those present would claim they could feel him thinking. The annals of history list many great thinkers—Archimedes, Newton, Einstein, Hawking. But for sheer concentrated brainpower, no one ever thought harder than Pietro Begnini did at that moment. He let his mind run free. Because he had learned what all those great thinkers eventually learned—that imagination is more powerful than knowledge.

Remember everything Vito taught you, he told himself. Take a deep breath. Exhale slowly. Release the tension in your shoulders. Close your eyes. Focus on a vibrant moment from your childhood. Expose yourself. Scrutinize your soul. Imagine you are flying. See the world from a distance. Obtain an objective viewpoint. Make your heart obey your instructions. Recall your mother, cradling your infant self in her arms. Recall your father, instructing you on the fundamentals of produce. Recall the first time you heard Sophia sing. Capture that love in your heart. Find a quiet place within yourself. Dig deeper....

And then he remembered the other lesson Vito taught him. Inspiration comes when you need it most.

He opened his eyes. "We must build a pipeline. Just as Leo would do. A pipeline to transport the water."

The Inquisitor stared at him incredulously. "No wonder you failed the Academy. You're a blithering idiot. Those people inside have an hour at best. Constructing a pipeline would take weeks, months even."

Pietro stared back at him through narrowed eyes. "I was speaking...metaphorically."

Twenty-Five

Pietro shoved the Inquisitor aside and raced back to the top of the campanile. He had an idea, but not one he could bring about himself. He needed help, lots of it. So he stood on the balcony and spoke to the people who remained below.

"Listen to me," Pietro said, and he repeated himself until the crowd quieted. "Our work is not done. We must save our beloved poets trapped inside."

"A fool's quest," the Inquisitor shouted back. "This is a time for prayer. Not false hopes and evil dreams."

Pietro spoke even more loudly than before. "Are we a city of quitters? No, we are the cradle of civilization, the birthplace of courage and valor. Will we let our most beloved artists perish without attempting to save them?"

One man shouted "No!" and a host of others followed. "We must trust the Inquisitor!" another shouted, but he was soon drowned out by another cry. "Listen to the vegetable vendor!"

"Good people of Florence!" the Inquisitor shouted. "Would you be misled by a man who"—he chuckled into his hand—"couldn't even graduate from the Academy? I am sure he would like to redeem himself for his many past failures. But I am your

Inquisitor and I question the authority of any man who would instill false hope for his own selfish purposes."

A new voice, a higher-pitched one, pierced the piazza. "You need to sit down and shut your lying mouth, Luigi. Inquisit that!"

This voice was Pietro's mother, Beatrice, and she'd had about as much of this nonsense as she was going to take.

The Inquisitor smiled at her. "Dear lady—"

"Don't Dear Lady me, Luigi. I remember when you were still a snot-nosed waif who tripped his brother when he wasn't look-ing. I didn't trust you then, I didn't trust you when you tried to keep my boy out of the Academy, and I don't trust you now."

"But Beatrice, please recall—"

"I know, you had a tough childhood. Grow up already. My boy, the one you ran off even though he's the best poet you ever laid eyes on, is trying to save those people. You're going to be quiet and get out of his way."

"Dear deluded lady, your son lies—"

She grabbed him by his robes. "My boy hasn't told a lie since he was thirteen years old and I hardly think he's going to start now. You on the other hand have a history of perfidy that perme-ates your entire life. So clam up or I tell everyone how you used to steal turnips from my husband's stand when you were a sniveling pup. Don't bother denying it, I have witnesses."

"But—"

She held up a finger. "Last chance."

The Inquisitor fell silent.

"Listen to me," Pietro shouted. He tried to recapture the crowd's attention, but many were leaving. Fewer and fewer could breathe so close to the billowing smoke. He knew that he must use his gifts to stir the people to action. What he was about to ask would be hard and fraught with risk. But he knew poetry had always inspired men and women to be better, to put others before themselves. He marshaled everything he knew, every-thing he had ever learned...

Anadiplosis. "We citizens of Florentine are thrice servants: servants of the state, servants of our families, and servants of one another." Asyndeton. "We are willing to pay any price, bear any burden, travel where no traveler has dared travel before." Catachresis. "We watch over one another with loving eyes." Metonymy. "We are people of language and inspiration, not easily satisfied, not content to be commonplace." Personification. "Florence expects everyone to do their duty to this still-breathing city. And that is why I call upon you now." Zuegma. "Not Florence's great sun, nor this night's great fire shall burn away the memory of what we do this day." Anaphora. "We shall not fail. We shall not flag. We shall not be anything but that which we were born to be." Aporia. "You may well wonder, what can I possibly do against this impenetrable inferno?" Climax. "Let me answer your question. We will do what must be done. We will strive, we will seek, and we will never yield. We will save our brethren, because in so doing, we save ourselves."

Pietro inhaled deeply, pressing his nightshirt to his mouth. He had their attention. Now he had to lead. That he would do with the simple words of a Florentine vegetable vendor, someone no different from anyone else.

"What I am about to ask will put you who have just emerged from danger back in harm's way. I do not ask it because it will be easy. I ask it knowing it will be hard. Hard work and personal risk require a special kind of people. But there are no people more special than we Florentines, yes?" A small murmur arose, then spread throughout the piazza. "Are we not people who cherish art and poetry above all else? While others obsess on the worst aspects of humanity, poetry celebrates its finest attributes. That is our shared heritage. We are not mere men and women. We are Florentines!" At this, the crowd replied with thunderous cheers. "Will we shirk from this challenge, those of us still on our feet despite this tainted air? We few, we happy few, we band of breathers? I think not!"

The crowd rallied. Fists flew into the air.

"My people, we must bring water to the auditorium to quench those flames. No pipeline exists. Therefore, we must create one. To put it more directly, we must become one. And this is how we will do it."

INSIDE THE RING OF FIRE, THE INTENSE HEAT AND BILLOWING SMOKE became virtually unendurable. Many of the people trapped inside, including Paolo's wife, had passed out. Even those still standing knew they did not have long to live. The fire had pushed them back against the rear wall with barely forty feet to maneuver.

Paolo was one of the few who remained alert. "I'm going up that wall," he said. "If I can get to the overhead walkway, I may be able to lower a rope."

"Don't do it," Georgio said. "The fire has weakened the wall supports."

"That may help. If the boards warp, it will create new foot or handholds. I'll take the bench as far as it goes, then scale the wall as best I can."

"You will crash to your death."

"I would rather die trying than die not trying,"

Georgio could not argue with his logic. He loaned Paolo his gloves so he would have some protection against the searing heat.

Paolo started his ascent. He could see flames lapping the top of the wall, near the walkway. His plan was doomed before it began.

He did it anyway.

LEADING THE TOWNSPEOPLE BEHIND HIM LIKE THE PIED PIPER, Pietro raced to the Arno and the fireboats docked there. The boatsmen were aware of the fire and stood ready, but they knew even their longest hoses would not reach the Tontino.

"Do you have buckets?" Pietro asked them.

"Yes," the leader of the boatsmen said. "But they can carry only—"

"How many buckets?"

He looked about. "Hundreds, but—"

"Start filling them."

Pietro stood on a raised dock and addressed the townspeople. "I want you to form a line. A tightly packed line, stretching all the way from here to the Tontino. You will be the pipeline—metaphorically speaking. We will pass the buckets along one by one. I want Romeo, our pitcher, he with the strongest arm, at the end. He will fling the water at the fire. We will put it out slowly but surely. Then we will retrieve our poets."

The townspeople stretched from the dock to the auditorium, almost a kilometer in length. The boatsmen filled each bucket and passed it to the first man in line, who passed it to the person beside him, who passed it to the person beside him…

GIANNOTTI PAUSED, JUST AT THE POINT WHEN I LEAST WANTED TO hear a pause. "You may realize that what Pietro formed was the first bucket brigade. Some histories erroneously identify the first bucket brigade as occurring in your country, in Philadelphia in 1736, when the Union Fire Company extinguished a tremendous fire using this technique under the direction of Benjamin Franklin. But after the conflagration was contained, when Dr. Franklin was asked where he got the idea, he answered, "It came to me like Florentine poetry." Some people thought this was a reference to sudden inspiration, or perhaps, a suggestion that reading poetry had triggered his imagination. But in truth, Franklin was indicating that he, like all learned men, knew the story of Pietro Begnini."

I arched an eyebrow. "You're saying Franklin cribbed from the Florentines?"

"My dear friend, everyone cribs from the Florentines."

PIETRO SUPERVISED HIS HUMAN PIPELINE, MAKING SURE EVERYONE did what they were supposed to do and that the water made its way to the auditorium. He knew they could not put out the fire altogether, but hoped they might create a passage for the people still trapped inside. As soon as the pipeline was functioning, he made his way back to the loading dock.

Pietro's Kongming lanterns were designed for transporting vegetables, not passengers. But Pietro, once again thinking metaphorically, had an idea. If he removed all the vegetables, the largest of his balloons might be able to lift him into the air. The tether would only take him as far as the vegetable stands. If he released the tether, he would be at the mercy of violent winds. The fire would likely draw the balloon to it—but he had no means of preventing the balloon from being incinerated. He could not hope to carry water to the flames. At best, he could carry ropes. He hoped to affix the ropes to the overhead walkway, to give those trapped below a means of escape.

Could he secure the ropes before the fire destroyed the balloon? And even if he did—how would he survive the inevitable fall once the balloon was destroyed?

This was a suicide mission.

He did not hesitate a moment before he climbed into the balloon and launched himself toward the inferno.

ONCE ALOFT, PIETRO OBSERVED THAT HIS HUMAN PIPELINE HAD already brought water to the flames. That was excellent news. But Pietro saw something else as well. One of the poets had attempted to climb the rear wall—and become trapped by fire, with no means of moving up or down.

Pietro cut the tether. The balloon was drawn inextricably toward the fire.

And as he neared, he realized the man trapped on the wall was Paolo.

You can imagine the thoughts racing through Pietro's head. This was the former friend who had stolen the woman he loved, the woman he was destined to be with throughout eternity. If Paolo perished—

Pietro put the thought out of his mind. He slowly released air from the balloon, causing it to descend. Flames crackled all around him. He tied both ropes to iron tethers on the walkway, one descending to safety, the other to the flaming pit below.

Just as he finished tying the second rope, the balloon caught fire.

Pietro plummeted. He jumped out of the flaming balloon, holding tight to the rope. He swung downward in midair, leveling out beside Paolo.

"Put your arms around my neck," he shouted.

Paolo shook his head. "The rope will not hold us both!"

"It will."

"How can you be sure?"

"Because it has to."

The boards crumbled beneath Paolo. This section of the wall would not last another minute.

"You would save me, Pietro? After all I've done to you?"

"I have a strong sense of irony. Now stop talking and put your arms around my neck."

Paolo did as he was told. Pietro pushed off against the wall, repelling and hauling at the same time, slowly ascending the upper five feet of the wall. The weight on Pietro's back was incredible. But these arms had been honed by hours of hauling water to a cave and serving in a soup kitchen and toting provisions through the desert and carrying vegetables to market. They did not fail him now.

Pietro hoisted them both to the narrow flat walkway. He showed Paolo the second rope. "This wall will not last much longer. Make your way down."

"I can't leave without—"

"Look." Pietro pointed toward the auditorium. The human pipeline had opened a path and the poets and their companions streamed out. Some had to be carried. All were blackened and choking. But they were alive.

Pietro followed Paolo down the rope, dodging the flames and ignoring the heat. When he was still twenty feet from the ground, the entire wall collapsed. Pietro jumped. He covered his head and landed on his feet, rolling sideways to cushion the blow.

The impact knocked the breath out of him. He closed his eyes. He had given everything he had and now there was nothing left. He felt himself drifting away...

Somewhere in the distance, he heard the voice of his father, Sal. "Pietro, speak to me! Speak!"

"I'm...dying."

He felt his father's hand clench his tightly. "This is the end?"

Pietro opened his eyes. "I just meant I'm really tired. Don't you know a metaphor when you hear it?"

Pietro pushed himself to his feet and followed his father to the piazza. Survivors huddled together, covering their mouths and pulling blankets tightly around themselves.

The Inquisitor milled through the crowd, acting concerned. "I knew if I kept pushing that boy, he would eventually amount to something. Enormous promise he had, you know. But intellectually lazy."

"I do not find him so," said Bernardo, the priest of the leading church in the district. "And I never did. And since it is almost Christmas Eve, Pietro, I would like to invite you to recite during the Christmas Eve service."

Pietro touched one hand to his chest. "Me? But—"

The priest cut him off. "You know how important this service is to the people of Florence. Everyone expects to hear from our greatest poets." He paused. "And one thing now is absolutely clear. There are no poets greater than you."

"I forbid it!" the Inquisitor said, throwing back his shoulders. "This man is no poet. He could not even graduate from the Academy. We will not sully our services with unskilled laborers."

The priest tilted his head. "Surely under the circumstances—"

"No," the Inquisitor insisted, "we must be rigorous. We must maintain our standards."

"I think we should make an exception in this case."

"Absolutely not. I control the performance of poetry in this town. And I forbid it."

"In that case," Paolo said, standing directly before the Inquisitor, "I won't be reciting either."

"Nor I," said Georgio, and one by one every poet who had been trapped in the fire, which was every poet in town, refused to recite.

"I see," the Inquisitor said. "We have a little rebellion on our hands. Fine. I will handle the Christmas Eve service myself."

"I think not," Father Bernardo said. "Because I have decided that the church will be closed. All day."

"On Christmas Eve? You can't do that."

"Of course I can," the priest sniffed. "Horrible plumbing problem. Needs immediate attention."

"As it happens," another priest said, "my church will be closed as well."

And so it went until at last, no poets would speak and no churches would be open on Christmas Eve.

"Fine," the Inquisitor said. "Then we will have no poetry in Florence at all."

"Of course we will." Sal stepped forward. "I meant to tell you before. I'm hosting a poetry reading tomorrow at my vegetable stand. And since it's my stand," he said, laying his hand on his son's shoulder, "I'm sure no one will object if I ask my favorite employee to recite."

"You are not licensed!" the Inquisitor shouted. "You are not a member of the Guild."

"And I never will be," Sal replied. "So you have no jurisdiction over me. I'm holding a poetry reading." He smiled. "With free vegetables."

The crowd cheered. The Grand Inquisitor stormed off in a huff, but Pietro did not notice, because in the distance, he spotted Paolo crouched down on one knee beside a bundled figure.

He slowly moved toward them. The cloth over her nose and mouth obscured her face.

Pietro hesitated. "This must be…your wife."

"It is."

"I'll leave you two—"

"Please do not go. I think she would like to see her savior."

Pietro crouched down and peered into her eyes. A moment later, he gently moved the cloth away from her face.

It was not Sophia.

Twenty-Six

The Christmas Eve reading started at the vegetable stand but eventually spread throughout the city to restaurants, bars, even the piazza where Pietro had once spoken on an upended vegetable box. In fact, the reading went about everywhere it could possibly go—except, of course, the churches. The Grand Inquisitor fumed but there was nothing he could do. All his threats and protestations had no impact on people who had just seen themselves and their city saved by the heroic efforts of the boy with the face of a doofus—and the courage of the world's greatest poet.

Christmas Day found Pietro high in the Tuscan hills, at a remote nunnery lodged on a sloped rise with very little to recommend it.

Barely forty-eight hours had elapsed since Pietro saved the city, but word of his deeds travelled well ahead of him. When he arrived at the doorstep, the Mother Superior knew exactly who he was and had a fairly good idea why he had come. Even though it was highly irregular, she admitted him and arranged the meeting he requested.

She was wrapped in the nun's hood and habit, but Pietro could see she had aged well. Her face was smooth and pure and she still seemed to shine with the illumination of the cherubim. Her voice was so musical it was as if she were singing each time she spoke.

"About time," she said.

Pietro stood before her, awkwardly fidgeting. "I gather you are not in fact married?"

"No, and I never was. After you failed your exam, my father demanded that I marry Paolo. I refused. He dragged me to Paolo's home and left me there, but I still refused. They called a priest, but I wouldn't cooperate. To save face, Paolo had the man conduct a false ceremony which many watched through the window, but no one was married. My father said I could marry Paolo or marry no one, so I chose the latter. Paolo left town to hide his embarrassment. When people asked about it, he lied. I understand he eventually married another. I moved here and I have remained here ever since."

"I came for you," Pietro said. "After I failed the examination."

"I know. I was already gone."

"Paolo told me he married you."

"He could not face the shame of rejection."

"He should have told me."

"I believe he regretted what he did, eventually. Why else would he return for the Calcio Storico? He knew you had returned to Florence. And he knew that as soon as everyone saw the face of his true wife—they would know the truth. Including you."

"I didn't see him. Not until the fire." Pietro took a few hesitant steps forward. "I hear your father has passed away."

She nodded. "Nine years now."

"I would've come sooner...if I'd realized you were here."

"I know."

"I'm still not a poet. Not officially."

"I know."

"I sell vegetables."

"I know."

"I—I really don't have much to offer…"

She reached out her hand. "You sweet silly doofus. My father cared about prestige and wealth. All I ever cared about was you."

His heart raced. "Then—you'll marry me?"

"Good grief, Pietro, I've been waiting a couple of decades. Of course I'll marry you."

And so the two were finally united as one person in the eyes of the courts and the church, but the truth was, they had been joined in the eyes of heaven from the day they met. The wedding was set for New Year's Day, appropriately enough, and it was the grandest wedding Florence had ever seen, not because the parties were rich but because almost everyone in town contributed. Everyone who had been saved from the inferno attended and many others as well. Machiavelli showed up, and Botticelli, and at the last minute, Leo arrived in something he called a gyrocopter, which truth be told, was not as sound in execution as it had looked on paper. Even Vito left his cave to attend the blessed event.

Pietro sent word to Rome for Lucy, but was told she had died while giving birth in her third and final arranged marriage. She was buried in the Convent of Corpus Domini. Pietro arranged to have flowers sent from the finest gardens in Rome, and once every year he visited her tomb and read her poetry.

The Grand Inquisitor did not attend the wedding, and even after that he did everything in his power to prevent Pietro from appearing publicly as a poet. But Pietro had saved the city, and perhaps even more importantly, he was a good boy, and a good town always rallies behind a good boy. Since the Inquisitor would not let Pietro recite during the Christmas Eve services, the churches remained closed on Christmas Eve, and all the poets in the city respected this decision because they respected Pietro.

Pietro and Sophia's lives were filled with bliss. Reunited with his great love, words flowed from Pietro in a poetic stream unparalleled at that time or any other. One moving, innovative, breathtaking poem followed another. Pietro wrote with the fire of an artist who finally knows what he is doing and why, with his beloved muse at his side. Sophia composed music for his poems and those songs were performed throughout the city. They had three children, all boys, and to this day Florence is said to be filled with the descendants of Pietro and Sophia, explaining perhaps why the city is so poetic and musical. The family even acquired a dog, though Beatrice was careful to put the young-sters in charge of its care, quietly informing Sophia that her husband did not have a great track record with canines.

Twelve years later, the Inquisitor passed away in his sleep one night, and Vito was given the Inquisitorship that should have been his years before. His first official act was to grant Pietro an honorary degree from the Academy, based upon his completion of his final exam by devising an original metaphor in the field of duty. After that, Pietro could appear in the churches on Christmas Eve, but by that time tradition had set in, and people were accustomed to going to strange places such as universities and bookstores and coffee shops to hear poetry recited.

Pietro and Sophia lived to advanced ages, as lovers often do. On the final day of his life, when he was bedridden and his vision was feeble, Pietro received an unexpected visitor.

Pietro peered up at the stranger with blurred eyes. "*You!* Have I been that terrible?"

"Indeed not."

Pietro squinted, trying to see more clearly. "You're the Evil One!"

The vision smiled. "That is what you called me, many years ago."

"You're the devil."

"I'm not."

"You tested me!" Pietro shouted toothlessly.

"If I had not, you would never have fulfilled your destiny."

"You cursed me!"

"I said you would never achieve your dreams until you were surrounded by the flames of hell. And that one turned out to be spot on, didn't it?"

Pietro batted his aged lips together. "If you are not the Evil One, then who are you?"

"I have many names and I couldn't care less which one people use."

"I have to call you something."

"Fine. Call me Inspiration."

"And why have you come to see me this day?"

"How could Inspiration not be with the world's greatest poet in his final moments?"

"I'm not the world's greatest poet."

"You are. And you worked hard for it, so don't waste your precious time with modesty."

"Am I going to die?"

"Never."

Pietro tried to lean forward. "Am I going to live forever?"

"Your poetry will."

"I haven't even published!"

"It's the work that matters, not the acclaim. Your greatest poetry is your life. You showed people what a poet can be, how a poet's life should be lived."

"I failed frequently."

"Because you tried to do so much."

"I made many mistakes."

"What first draft was ever worth reading? But a great poet doesn't quit there, does he? The great poet revises. Keeps working till he gets it right."

"Did I...get it right?"

"Not at first. But in time, you got past your own cleverness and discovered what truly matters. And then you were ready to be a poet. You were ready to teach others how to see what they did not see before."

Pietro settled back into his pillow. "Am I going somewhere nice?"

"Indeed. A place where poetry is everywhere."

"What about Sophia?"

"This is your reward, not hers."

"I'm not going anywhere without her." He folded his arms across his chest. "A poet is nothing without his muse."

"You have become wise indeed, Pietro. And so you pass your final examination." The vision took him by the hand and gently lifted him upward. "Time to go."

Twenty-Seven

"And with that," Giannotti announced, "we have at last reached the conclusion of my story." I heard cathedral bells chiming. "And not a moment too soon. It is almost midnight."

He glanced at Chiara. She buttoned her coat and headed toward the stairs.

"Good night," Giannotti said, waving. "I hope your performance goes well. Happy Christmas."

"And to you. Both of you." She disappeared from sight.

"I'm assuming there's some reason you told me this tale," I said. The night air rushed into my lungs and I felt lightheaded. "Other than explaining that the churches are closed in tribute to the poet who saved the city. You could have given me that in a few sentences. Why the historical epic?"

"It is my job to look after my guests. When I first saw you here on the terrace, you looked unhappy. Frightened."

"More like terrified. I've got writer's block. The permanent kind. I've lost the words."

"But you are an educated man. You know many words. What does it mean, this writer's block? No one gets plumber's block. Why should a writer?"

"Writer's block means—" I stopped and thought a moment. "It means you don't know what to say."

"How can a poet not have anything to say? When the world is so filled with wondrous material?"

"I—I wrote a poem a few years ago. It became very famous."

"Yes. 'The Other Door.' About your mother. You mentioned it."

"Before that, I was successful, but most people had no idea who I was or what I did. After the huge acclaim that poem received..." I stopped weighing each word before I spoke and just let the thoughts tumble out. "...after that, it was almost as if I was competing with myself. I would write, but nothing ever seemed any good. Certainly not as good as 'The Other Door.' People said I was the best poet in the world. But when I looked at what I wrote—it just didn't measure up."

"Ahh." Giannotti steepled his fingers. "You were trying to be the greatest poet in the world—a difficult standard to meet. What did Pietro learn when he was tempted in the desert with the promise of being the best? The need to be best drove the Inquisitor to a heinous act that almost obliterated Florence. Perhaps, my friend, you should forget about being the best. Perhaps you should give yourself permission to be only... say...47th."

Something clicked inside my head.

"Some fairly distinguished poets have done no better," Giannotti continued. "Time for you to start fresh. To be the little boy who scribbled four-line doggerel on the back of a church bulletin to please his mother. After all, you can always improve it later, true? As Pietro learned, no one gets it right on the first attempt. Writing is about revision—just as life is."

I remained silent.

"Every time you start anew, you are a beginner."

I craned my neck. "Okay, now you've lost me."

"Forgive me, but in my many years at this Palazzo, I like to believe I have learned a little something about people. I do not need a polygraph to reveal truths that are visible simply by peering into someone's eyes." He gave me a gentle yet penetrating stare. "You did not break up with your girlfriend before you came to Florence, did you?"

I saw no point in perpetuating the façade. "No."

"There never was any girlfriend, was there?"

"No." I inhaled deeply, letting the night air fill me. "When I wrote 'The Other Door,' I was grieving over the loss of my mother, the woman I loved more than anything, the one who praised my first poem, the only person who thought I could succeed as a writer. And then—"

Giannotti's hand fell on my shoulder.

My face scrunched up and I found I could not speak without a tremble. "I loved that woman. God, how I loved her. She believed in me even when I didn't believe in myself. I know, I should get over it. But I can't. I *can't*. I miss her. And I'm so embarrassed about it that I invented a breakup with a girlfriend who never existed to explain why I'm so…scared. And… empty."

"What was Pietro searching for all those years? What did he need before he could write great and original poetry? Your mother was a wonderful woman but she was not destined to be with you forever. You must find the one you are missing."

"I'm not good at meeting people."

"This I believe. But love will come your way. Do not be blind when it arrives."

"I'm not blind to—"

I froze.

"Love is all around you," Giannotti continued. "Especially at Christmastime. Pay attention. Before it's too late."

"But—But—"

"Go. Now."

I jumped out of my seat and raced down the narrow staircase as fast as I could possibly move. I ran into the street, snowflakes pelting me in the face.

She was performing somewhere. But where? It was a church. She mentioned a church. But which one? There were so many, and now they all had their doors opened wide...

I ran down the via del Serragli, darting into one church after another, searching. Church after church after church, jostling through the crowds, dodging hundreds of people. I saw laughter and gaiety everywhere, but in my heart there was only a feeling of stupidity, of the certain knowledge that I had been given a gift, a Christmas present, and allowed it to slip away.

With each moment I grew more desperate. For all I knew, her performance was over and the moment had passed and—

"Are you lost?"

I whirled around. Chiara stood behind me. She carried a violin case and a leather satchel.

"I found you!" I cried.

"I told you I was playing tonight." She gestured toward the open church doors. "Right in there. Is that not why you are here?"

It seemed like it took me forever to gather my wits. "Yes. That's exactly why I'm here."

She smiled. "I know I have been popping up every time you turned around today. But—" She blew a snowflake off her nose. "May I make a small confession?"

"I'm no priest. Actually, I'm—"

"I know who you are. I knew who you were when I checked you in. I've read everything you've ever written."

"Meaning, you've read 'The Other Door?'"

"No, everything." She opened her satchel, revealing copies of every one of my books. "*Painting by Numbers. Percy Revisited. The Trouble with Words. Reflections on a Blade of Grass. Two Coins Too Many. The Clock That Ticks the Time.* Two copies of *Syllables from the Afterlife,* because it's my favorite. Sometimes. I even bought your *Selected Poems,* though I already had every poem in it. In fact, I think I've memorized every poem in it. I have one of them mounted on my refrigerator. I named my cat for one of your poems! I've wanted to talk to you since the first moment you checked in and kept making foolish attempts to initiate a conversation. I think you are the best poet in—"

"I'm not the best poet," I said, cutting her off. "I don't have to be the best. I just have to write. Write and write and do the best work I can."

"Your work is so extraordinary. How did it start? How did you begin writing poetry?"

I felt a sudden tugging behind my eyes. I pulled the locket out of my pocket, the locket I always carried, and opened it. On one side was a scrap of a poem written by a seven-year old on the back of a church bulletin. On the other side was a black-and-white photo of my young mother holding her baby boy. We gazed at one another, eyes bright and glistening.

"Your mother loved you very much," Chiara said.

"It was all because of her." I brushed my hand across my eyes. "That's why it was so hard to continue after she was gone."

"But—do you not see? She isn't gone." Chiara reached into her satchel and pulled out my *Selected Poems*. "She lives right here. And she always will."

I squeezed the locket all the tighter.

Her cheeks flushed. "I tried to work up the courage to speak to you," she said, "but I didn't want you to think I was a dangerous stalker poet groupie. So I left you alone."

"Until today."

She squirmed. "No one should be alone on Christmas Eve."

"Absolutely correct." I pointed at the violin case. "Didn't Gianotti say you compose music as well as play it?"

"I try. I have some decent melodies. But I'm no good with words. I hope you will not hate me but—I have set some of your poems to music. I know, hideous copyright infringement, very criminal. But I have not published them or put them on YouTube—"

"No, no," I said, cutting her off. "I think that's…wonderful. I —I think…" I inhaled deeply, steeling myself with the night air. "I think we should consider collaborating. Is it too late to accept your invitation to the concert?"

"I would welcome your company. I always go to this service,

every year, even if I am not playing. I have always loved church at Christmastime. I was dating this man who did not like Christmas or anything to do with it. He wanted to marry me, but I could never marry a man who did not like Christmas."

Something echoed in the back of my brain. "Of course not. This is the season of miracles."

She smiled. "Every day is a miracle. You just have to open your eyes and see all the wonders the angels have brought you."

A chill raced up my spine, and then, a moment later, I was filled with the most intense warmth, and the greatest certainty, I have ever known.

She glanced sideways toward the open doors. "Shall we go inside?"

"Yes. Definitely."

Chiara left her satchel with me and took her violin to the choir loft. Before the service began, I placed the locket inside her copy of my *Selected Poems*, put it back in the satchel, and closed my eyes.

Thank you, Mother. For everything.

And then I took out my pen, turned over the church bulletin, and began to write.

William Bernhardt is the author of over sixty books, including *The Last Chance Lawyer* (#1 *National Bestseller)*, the historical novels *Challengers of the Dust* and *Nemesis*, three books of poetry, and the Red Sneaker series of books on writing. In addition, Bernhardt mentors aspiring authors, hosts an annual conference (WriterCon), small-group seminars, a newsletter, and a bi-weekly podcast.

Bernhardt has received the Southern Writers Guild's Gold Medal Award, the Royden B. Davis Distinguished Author Award (University of Pennsylvania) and the H. Louise Cobb Distinguished Author Award (Oklahoma State), which is given "in recognition of an outstanding body of work that has profoundly influenced the way in which we understand ourselves and American society at large." In 2019, he received the Arrell Gibson Lifetime Achievement Award from the Oklahoma Center for the Book.

In addition Bernhardt has written plays, a musical (book and score), humor, children stories, biography, and puzzles. He has edited two anthologies (*Legal Briefs* and *Natural Suspect*) as fundraisers for The Nature Conservancy and the Children's Legal Defense Fund. In his spare time, he has enjoyed surfing, digging for dinosaurs, trekking through the Himalayas, paragliding, scuba diving, caving, zip-lining over the canopy of the Costa Rican rain forest, and jumping out of an airplane at 10,000 feet.

In 2017, when Bernhardt delivered the keynote address at the San Francisco Writers Conference, chairman Michael Larsen noted that in addition to penning novels, Bernhardt can "write a sonnet, play a sonata, plant a garden, try a lawsuit, teach a class, cook a gourmet meal, beat you at Scrabble, and work the *New York Times* crossword in under five minutes."

About the Illustrator

I have always loved to draw. I began my career in fifth grade when they put me in accelerated math to work on my own. I never worked on math a day after that, until I was found out. I spent my time drawing pictures and I would sell them to kids at lunch time.

I attended Rick College and began my education. I continued learning at Brigham Young University-Provo. I now live in Ammon, Idaho, with my wife and family and work as an illustrator. I'm represented by illustrationonline.com. I also share my talents and love of art as an instructor at Brigham Young University-Idaho.

Brian Call

Also by William Bernhardt

The Daniel Pike Novels

The Last Chance Lawyer

Court of Killers

Trial by Blood

Twisted Justice

Judge and Jury

Final Verdict

The Splitsville Novels

Splitsville

Exposed

Shameless

The Ben Kincaid Novels

Primary Justice

Blind Justice

Deadly Justice

Perfect Justice

Cruel Justice

Naked Justice

Extreme Justice

Dark Justice

Silent Justice

Murder One

Criminal Intent

Death Row

Dazzling Description: Painting the Perfect Picture

The Fundamentals of Fiction (video series)

Poetry

The White Bird

The Ocean's Edge

Traveling Salesman's Son

For Young Readers

Shine

Princess Alice and the Dreadful Dragon

Equal Justice: The Courage of Ada Sipuel

The Black Sentry

Edited by William Bernhardt

Legal Briefs: Short Stories by Today's Best Thriller Writers

Natural Suspect: A Collaborative Novel of Suspense

Christmas Tapestry: A Collection of Holiday Tales

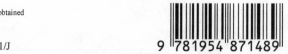